AFTER LIFE: INFERNO

BOOK ONE

ROBERT CHAZZ CHUTE

PRAISE FOR ROBERT'S WORK

Chute sucks you in from word one and pulls you down his post apocalyptic rabbit hole! You will sleep with the lights on, covers pulled over your head and dust off the old teddy bear for comfort. Horrifically well written and engaging. There are other popular books in this genre, but after reading this there is nothing else that climbs to the heights of Chute's caliber. Chazz ranks among the top tier of our generation's storytellers. ~ Alex Kimmell, Author of *The Key to Everything*

Robert Chazz Chute is such a skilled spinner of tales that the reader is more than willing to suspend any possible disbelief to go along for the ride. ~ David Pandolfe, author of *Jump When Ready*

It's not very often one finds a writer with such a dark side that has such a great sense of humor. ~ Glenn Roberts, Amazon reviewer

The author has a definite talent with words and ideas. ~ Love to Read!, Amazon reviewer

His words lift and dance off the page, bringing the story to life. ~ Kindle Customer, Amazon reviewer

The world building is horrifically well done with twists and turns and deceit around every corner. ~ Wanda, Amazon reviewer

RCC blends characters' beliefs & worries concerning society's failures, plus vivid action scenes skillfully. ~ RMerkl, Amazon Reviewer

Nothing but sheer exhaustion could tear my eyes from the captivating dance of words choreographed by Robert Chazz Chute. ~ Halph Staph, Amazon reviewer

Wonderful action constantly holds your interest. ~ Sharon Finn, Amazon reviewer

The complexity and attention to detail throughout absolutely blow me away. ~ Kindle customer, Amazon Reviewer

Very few authors impress me with their actual writing style, it's usually always about the story. But this author paints such beautiful vivid pictures with words that I found myself not only enjoying the story but enjoying the way the words created images in my mind. I know that sounds corny, but it is true. ~ B.H., Amazon reviewer

Chute gives us story worthy of Stephen King. A read both thoughtful and fun. ~ Linda Beer Johnson, Amazon reviewer

The author does an excellent job building the characters and getting you invested and involved. ~ Michele L. Hebert, Amazon reviewer

I just can't say in words what a powerful author this is! ~ Delinda L. Calkins, Amazon reviewer

Robert Chazz Chute writes so skillfully as to make the supernatural seem perfectly logical - and terrifying! There are twists, turns and surprises galore. You will be glad you bought this book - until you lose sleep because you can't put it down. ~ johligo, Amazon reviewer

When I want to read apocalyptic books or zombie stories, those books have to also be extremely well-written and something that I could recommend with zeal and confidence to everyone I know. Robert Chazz Chute's books are exactly that. ~ Mazie Lane, Amazon reviewer

He makes the stuff that is obviously fiction, believable. ~ W. Nickels, Amazon reviewer

I am a lover of paranormal, dystopian novels and depth of story as well as intelligence in writing style, and Robert has it all. Humor, wit, depth, intelligence and an awesome way with words/writing. ~ Amazon Customer, Amazon reviewer

Each book of the NEXT Apocalypse Series
is also available individually in paperback as well as ebook. You can also
read the box set, bundled as an ebook.

AFTER Life INFERNO

AFTER Life PURGATORY

AFTER Life PARADISE

Special thanks to Gari Strawn for her excellent editorial services at
strawnediting.com.

Cover design by Rocking Book Covers

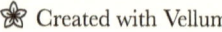 Created with Vellum

YOU MAY ALSO ENJOY

This Plague of Days, Omnibus Edition

and

Robot Planet, The Complete Series,

available in ebook and paperback.

You will find a full listing of books by this author at the end of this book.

AFTER LIFE INFERNO

CHAPTER TWO

WELCOME TO BOOK ONE

OF AFTER LIFE

INFERNO

EPISODE 1

AFTER (acronym)

Artificial Facilitation Therapy for Enhanced Response, a biomimetic stem cell nanotechnology with numerous health and wellness applications. The term was first coined by Chloe T. Robinson, PhD, a biomedical engineer at the University of Toronto, in 2013.

~ Notes from NEXT

1

My name is Daniel Harmon. This is my confession.

About a month into my duty on the Emergency Task Force, Steve Taylor told me about the building they called the Box. The way he talked about it sounded like a typical cop story. I told myself there might be a nugget of truth at the story's root but it was probably surrounded by a healthy dose of exaggeration. I was new to the Toronto Police Service's ETF and was wary of becoming the gullible noob who got hazed. The only reason I knew there was some truth to it was Taylor made sure I wouldn't talk to anybody outside the team about any possible mission we'd have there. I treated the Box as if it was a rumor that had gotten out of hand. Then one summer day we got the call.

"Green 32. Code Green 32 to the Box." It wasn't the regular dispatcher who gave the order. I recognized the Sergeant-Major's voice. I'd met her only twice, once when I graduated from training and again when I was interviewed to join the ETF.

As I pulled on Hazardous Materials gear, I asked Frank Barnes about the call. Frank was a sniper in the Forces before joining the ETF. He'd been promoted to Staff Sergeant two years ago. He was one of the older guys but he was friendly in a gruff way. He didn't look up as he pulled on his blue biohazard suit. "Some of the usual rules of engagement may not apply on this job."

"The guys told me bits and pieces about the Box. It's kind of an open secret, sir."

"Open secret, huh? Supposed to be only one kind of secret. What do you think you know?"

I shrugged. "I didn't think there was such a thing as a virus lab in a city. I thought they put them a thousand miles from nowhere in the bottom of abandoned salt mines or something. Then, during Hurricane Harvey, I heard there's a similar lab in Houston. It almost went down during the flood — "

Frank was more gruff than friendly this time. "We don't know shit yet and I won't know shit until I get there. You'll never know shit, clear?"

"Yessir."

He looked at me with hard, glassy eyes. "This is the deep water, Danny boy. Just watch my back and I'll do the heavy lifting." As Barnes pulled his tac belt around his waist, he moved like a man operating on automatic. His mind was elsewhere. His body was going through the motions. I'd seen him do recon, line up shots and console hostages. He was the kind of guy who wouldn't panic even as he was drowning. Still, I could tell by his face he wasn't prepared for Green 32. I'm sure now he never believed the order would ever come.

None of us really believed the rumors about the Box until we were in it. Then it was too late.

On the ride to the scene in the back of the Hazardous Materials truck, there was no chatter among the guys. I found myself revisiting the absurdity of placing a dangerous disease research lab in the middle of a city. If there is ever a hearing about how our disaster unfolded, I suspect it'll be like the Fukushima nuclear disaster inquiries. Why did they construct a nuclear reactor over a fault line? Why did they build a nuclear plant in a spot vulnerable to tsunamis?

After everything goes bad, answers to those questions are not satisfying. All we'll get is excuses, talking in circles, helpless shrugs. The tallies of the casualties climb until the media gets bored of the sensational. People keep dying but no one pays attention. If one pretty little girl disappears or is killed, they won't let that story die. Kill off a lot of people and people become casual about death.

Casual about death? Maybe that's why they're called casualties.

Maybe they built a viral research center in the middle of Toronto because they couldn't persuade the best virologists to work in Antarctica. After a hard day sweating in biohazard suits, the nice doctors studying the most dangerous bugs in history wanted to pop over to the Eaton Centre for a frozen yogurt. Perhaps the allure of Philosopher's Walk over at U of T was too much for them. I love Queen's Park in the fall, too. All well and good until somebody gets sloppy and breaches Level 4 containment. We knew the Box held the most dangerous viruses in the world. We had no idea it contained the very worst of something new and different.

None of the why of things matters much now. We're beyond the why and the how. Life's all about the next meal, finding shelter for the night and not getting bitten. We don't have a time machine to go back and stop the contagion. Just because it's too late doesn't mean we can't assign blame. The trouble is, I'm to blame for opening Pandora's Box.

The scientists froze the test tube nightmares in the deepest lab: anthrax, ebola, rabies, various poxes. The rumor was that above the elevator to Level 4 a sign read: *Abandon all hope, ye who enter here.* Somebody had a sense of humor. But it wasn't entering the Box that caused the end of the world. Getting out was the problem.

Staff Sergeant Barnes once shot a guy who took hostages on a TTC bus on Bay Street. I'd never killed before. I'd had to pull my weapon many times as a beat cop. I'd been in a lot of fights but I'd never killed anyone. I never thought I'd be put in the position of shooting people running at me in lab coats.

Once the regular uniforms had secured the perimeter, we'd go in wearing our biohazard suits. Barnes told us our job was to secure the Box and keep a lid on it. I'd hated training in our blue environmental suits. They were meant for dealing with chemical spills or "other mass casualty scenarios involving biohazards." They were bulky, the hood was heavy and they were too hot. The canned air strapped to our backs smelled sweet at first, but after a few minutes in the suit, I felt claustrophobic and sweaty.

As we pulled to a stop, I asked the Staff Sergeant, "How do we know who's infected?"

"Until further notice, assume they all are," Barnes replied. "I'll take point and do the interviewing. The rest of you hang back and control the scene."

The guys on the team threw around the term *zombie* a lot. They were trying to be funny. I've grown up around cops all my life. We all have at least a touch of gallows humor. You have to if you want to try to stay sane for all the shit you see. I've seen beaten dogs and dead babies. I've seen people in their worst moments doing the worst things imaginable. It was natural to call the infected by the z-word, just like we referred to terrorists as tangos. Killing terrorists was *slotting tangos*. We used those terms because you don't want to think of an enemy as a human being suffering any problem you might understand. Dehumanization is necessary to do our job, to stay detached, to be professional. If you got into every sob story, you couldn't police the offenders. I've got weapons of death and torture on my belt. I used to say things like, "I'm a cop, not a social worker." I said it with pride and a smile.

Things became more complicated after we got in the Box. I wanted to think what happened was the scientists' own damn fault for working there, for somehow letting the genie out of the bottle. Now, through sleepless nights, I lie very still and wonder how many mistakes led us to the apocalypse.

Barnes told us we could be dealing with a variant of rabies. People could lose their minds. They might run fast or they might walk funny and fall down a lot. They could bite and tear our suits, "compromising our barrier to possible infection." The infected might have a fever or foam at the mouth. "They might even seem fine at first," he warned us.

We should have known better. Every civilization falls eventually but this one's on me. All that death was my fault.

2

The employees who weren't trapped below Level 1 got out of the Box before we arrived. Witnesses said some ran toward the subway. Others fled into PATH, downtown Toronto's underground shopping network. The tunnels and walkways spread over thirty kilometers. It is a rabbit warren built so shoppers could avoid Toronto's punishing winter winds and multiply the number of places to buy expensive things. Each fleeing employee would have to be tracked down. People on the run always run home. Every person they talked to or touched would have to be quarantined and monitored.

On such a beautiful July day, abandoning the sunshine to work underground seemed extra sad. For us, going deep into the Box felt like running into the dragon's den. Once we arrived, it was as if a clock had been set in motion, its gears and cogs spinning, the numbers counting down to zero.

I've replayed that afternoon in my head a hundred different ways. The Box was broken from the start because the incident began with a very loud alarm. The high grating tone pulsed on and on, harsh enough to rattle eardrums. Because of that damn alarm, every scenario ends in the same shit storm. If things had gone a different way, we could have corralled all the lab's employees in short order. They could have prepared us for what waited for us in the bowels of the complex. We might even have had the wisdom to seal off the building and leave it alone.

We could hear the alarm blaring as we rolled up. Staff Sergeant Gregory "Mac" MacGonigle, the incident commander, waited for us by his truck. We piled out of the back of the Hazardous Materials van ready to roll, respirators ready and comm gear already checked.

Mac didn't look at us. He spoke only to Staff Sergeant Barnes. "Frank, the people you have to concern yourself with are in the basement levels. Anybody past the front door could be infected and should be dealt with accordingly."

Our bomb tech, Bob Lundsden, asked Mac, "Do we have the layout of the place, Staff Sergeant?"

"Your team leader has it in his head," Mac replied. "Follow his lead."

It was a good question and standard procedure to find out what we were getting ourselves into. The Staff Sergeant brushed it off as if Lundsden had asked if his mom was available for a hot date.

"All you guys need to know is there are four levels: 1, 2, 3, 4. Got it? Your orders are to secure the location."

The first principle of operational security is to recognize who needs to know what and when they need to know it. I thought at the time that sending us in blind was dumb. It didn't occur to me my superiors weren't dumb. Their tactics were calculated.

All ten of us turned to head into the Box but Mac called us back. We surrounded him, listening carefully. I hoped Mac was about to give us a wink and tell us this was a drill. Instead, Mac looked from man to man for a moment before turning to our team leader. "It's bound to be cramped quarters in there. Can you do the job with four, Frank?"

It was a question that wasn't a question. A suggestion from Mac was an order. Cramped quarters or not, we'd pulled perps out of crawlspaces and spider holes. All of us should have gone in. Barnes and Mac had served together for years and knew each other well.

Our team leader could have used that relationship to make sure the whole team tackled the task. It went the wrong way. Some silent understanding seemed to pass between them. Staff Sergeant Barnes bobbed his head and chose the insertion team. He pointed to Bob Lundsden, Steve Taylor, Patrick Davis and me.

Since bombs weren't today's issue, Lundsden shouldered the battering ram in case we needed to break down an office door. Taylor, Davis and I were assaulters. I was hoping to get into the negotiator training program but was stuck on a waiting list.

We were the youngest members on the squad. None of us had wives or children. That should have rung alarm bells in my head. I didn't think about it at the time. This was just another call and I'd worked many calls that week. I figured I'd do my job and be back to my apartment that night, maybe go for a drink at the Loose Moose, maybe meet someone. Routines can rock you to sleep. Too much of the usual can make anyone miss the important clues when the unusual is about to kick your ass. Certainly the population of Toronto — nearly six million of us — went about their daily drag with no idea killer viruses could boil out of a pit beneath our city.

Still, I was sure Barnes was the best man to lead us into Hell. A nurse I dated once told me that her IQ points went up as soon as she put on her uniform. "Once I put on my scrubs, I speak differently. I'm a professional and tons more confident."

I didn't think to question the science behind her assertion. Since then it has occurred to me that speaking confidently sure sounds smarter but maybe isn't. In my uniform, surrounded by my buddies on the ETF squad, I got dumber. We didn't stand a chance. We didn't know that yet. Nobody comes back from Hell.

This door to Hell sported an unassuming sign. In small blue letters on a white field, the sign read: *Echidna Biosystems.* It looked like any other business, maybe less so since the sign was so small. Sometimes Evil hides in plain sight. People doing shady shit enjoy a low profile.

"The rest of the team stays with me," Mac said. "Push the perimeter back another block. I don't want anybody coming out of the bank across the street or any other building within the perimeter.

Once the insertion squad is into Level 2, we'll look at evacuating the area." He pointed at the office windows in the glass cubes and towers above us. "We still got a buncha gawkers on this side but the building's being emptied out above the second floor by the fire department. We're getting them out on t'other side of the building, onto Dundas. You guys focus on securing this side. We go where the trouble is. Nobody comes out of that door until the location is secure."

I glanced up at the tower of glass and steel spiking the sky above us and wondered how long it would take to evacuate all the civilians. Did they even suspect the devils in the basement? Did they ever wonder why their building lacked a parking garage? I bet some head of an accounting firm petitioned whoever owned the building a couple of times a year to get more parking under the building. Nobody knows what they don't know.

Underneath our hoods, our respirators connected to the long, slim oxygen tanks on our backs. Barnes gave the order for us to check our meters and oxygen flow one more time. We started with one hour and five minutes of reserve under normal circumstances but, of course, normal did not apply here. We'd already spent seven minutes of that out in the sunshine.

"Harmon," the Staff Sergeant said. "You good at math? You better be because you're the squad's oxygen clock. Keep an eye on your meter and the time. We take too long on any one level, sound off. Our lives are in your hands so don't go cross-eyed on me."

I was starting to perspire standing around in the sun but the added responsibility made me sweat more. I'd never been that great at math, and if we didn't get in and out quick, we'd be floppy fish gasping on a dock. We'd turn blue and die but we'd still have plenty of time to think about the horror of our deaths before everything went black. I checked my oxygen meter a lot while I was in the Box but it turned out to be less important than expected. We're always worrying about the wrong things.

Staff Sergeant Barnes gave us the signal to saddle up. I fell in behind him and put a hand on his shoulder. Taylor put a hand on my shoulder and so on. Barnes led the way across the street with his ballistic shield up. *POLICE* was emblazoned across the middle of the shield. Above the viewport was printed the word: *INTRUDER*. It was a weird quirk of branding to use that word on a fourteen hundred dollar shield used by the ETF. Looking back, it was appropriate. We were intruders into another world we didn't understand. Give me a simple hostage situation any day and I'll know what to do. Killer germs are, as Mac would say, "a whole nother."

Each man on the squad carried the MP5A3, a kickass submachine gun that made me feel taller. The July heat scorched into my dark blue biohazard suit. I wished I'd had a drink of water before I pulled the respirator over my face. I always drank less than I needed while I worked, though. It wouldn't do to have to pee when the shit hit the ceiling fan. My nose itched but of course I couldn't scratch it. I did my best to get at the itch by contorting my face. Didn't work.

As if he read my mind, Barnes said, "If you're ever of a mind to take off your mask and get some fresh air, keep in mind that death by asphyxiation is a mercy compared to what they got in the basement. We'll get in and out with at least fifteen minutes to spare on our oxygen supply."

I wondered how many employees the Staff Sergeant intended to interview. How could he be done that quick? I contented myself with the knowledge that my superiors had a plan. On paper, somehow their plan made sense to them. But does anything important ever go according to plan?

3

I've learned a lot since we went into the Box, but I didn't believe Frank then. Asphyxiation sounded like a terrible way to go compared to dying slow on clean white sheets in a hospital somewhere. I'd take all the drugs the doctors would give me and I'd fade away. I want what everybody wants. If I can't have an easy immortality, I'd prefer the sweet, painless kind of death where you go to sleep and you never wake up.

Even that deal can go bad, of course. People say, "He went peacefully in his sleep at home." That's usually a comforting lie. When I was a beat cop, I attended to plenty of dead body calls. If the DB came in early in the morning, the results were almost predictable. Some poor Personal Support Worker, a maid or a relative would discover the dead body in bed.

If the deceased was elderly and cold, we'd call for a hearse instead of an ambulance. If the body was warm and there was no DNR order, the paramedics might arrive in time to attempt to raise the dead. Whoever discovered the body would be upset, especially if they'd never seen a body outside of a funeral home. The dead don't look peaceful. Their slack faces appear long and horsey. Their eyes look drunk.

I've lied to a lot of distraught old widows, sons and daughters. "He went peacefully in his sleep."

The deceased's clawed hands, frozen in agony, betrayed my lies. Rumpled sheets and the blankets on the floor tell a story of a painful, lonely death.

The living look for solace in the stupidest places. When people die at work, inevitably someone will say, "Well, he died with his boots on."

Weird and empty. Dying barefoot on a beach by a tropical ocean while getting laid sounds much better to me.

Another favorite is, "She died doing what she loved."

She died under her desk clutching at her chest and trying to get to the phone!

With ordinary horrors as powerful as these, why did we have to go looking for trouble in test tubes?

As we approached the building, a small woman in a lab coat appeared in the doorway to the Box. She looked about forty. Her hair was mussed and she appeared dazed. Perhaps dazzled by the sunshine, she looked up at the sky. As she turned, I saw blood had soaked through her long lab coat down her right side, from her waist to her calf. Crimson blood dripped from her mouth.

"She needs EMS," Lundsden called out from the back of our line. "Call EMS!"

Ordinarily, he wouldn't be wrong. The woman looked like the victim of a vicious attack, one that might soon bleed out. Blood makes up seven percent of our body weight, about 5.5 liters. When it ranges outside the confines of our meatbags, though — sticky and smeared and flowing everywhere — it sure looks like a lot more than that.

We advanced toward her. "Ma'am?" Frank called. "Get back inside! Back inside!"

His command seemed give the woman focus. She peered at us, unmoving for a moment. I saw no fear in her eyes. I saw no expression at all. That blank expression was what made her so scary. I'd seen that before in victims and perps. Blood loss gives people that look. Certain drugs will do it, too. Sometimes it's the crazy gaze of someone with nothing left to lose. (I have that look now, I'm certain.)

I attended a call in the Jane Finch corridor once. We'd been to the same house several times over the course of six months or so. Domestic abuse calls are rarely one and done. The abuser always keeps a key and the victim often can't afford to change the locks. After relationships go sour, somebody gets kicked out. Then they make the mistake of coming back for love or their clothes, an old CD collection or a rice cooker.

I thought I knew the man at that familiar address well. I'd already arrested him once. His wife had filed for divorce but, unfortunately, she'd lost her resolve and did the kind thing. She gave him one more chance. When I walked in, she was on the floor, bloody, crying and pleading for help. Trying to speak through broken lips, missing teeth and possible brain damage, she was nearly incoherent.

The husband had been a big talker when I arrested him the first time, but cooperative enough. He looked like an old wrestler gone to seed. I told him to turn around and put his hands on his head. My plan was to get him out of the small apartment and away from the victim. Once I'd walked him backwards and into the hall, I would get him on the ground and cuffed. He had other plans.

I was pulling out my baton as he ran at me and pinned me to the wall. Instinctively, I threw an elbow across his jaw. He didn't seem fazed. I clocked him across the jaw again but all he did was grunt. He didn't begin to go down until I got a knee in his groin and my baton in his throat.

That man stared at me the same way this woman in the lab coat stared at us. There was no passion or anger. There was nothing to see or understand in those empty gazes. If we aren't careful, anyone can end up in a situation where we act on automatic. Circumstances can too easily turn us into unthinking murder and suicide machines, dead on the inside.

The woman ignored Barnes and stepped further into the sunshine.

Over his bullhorn, Mac commanded us to flatten. The squad went down on our stomachs.

"Send it, Crenshaw," Mac said.

A shot rang out.

18

Behind us, someone screamed.

The woman in the lab coat opened her mouth as if to speak. More blood poured out of her mouth as her body went loose, boneless. Before her face hit the concrete steps with a sickening wet smack, I saw the neat hole in the middle of her forehead.

I looked back. Dale Crenshaw, our team's second-best sniper, was positioned prone atop our van. He was still looking down his scope and he seemed to be staring at me.

4

————————

The Box was an anonymous bunker at the bottom of an office building in a sea of similar edifices. Across the street, a gaggle of civilians watched from behind the glass of a Royal Bank of Canada. As we made our way toward the front door I glanced back. Bank staff and customers jockeyed for position to get a better look. Some were pressed against the glass as if the bank's atrium was an overcrowded aquarium. I had that odd sensation of being stared at by strangers. What would they think if they knew one of the most dangerous virology labs in North America sat across the street all this time? And how messed up was it that there are many such labs? Each one is one mistake away from disaster. A dropped Petri dish, a faulty freezer coupling, a broken meter, one bad hire? So many variables, so many ways to go wrong. I've never owned a single car that didn't fail me at some point.

The first thing Mac did was shut down the Toronto Transit Commission. I found that out later. It sounds mean, doesn't it? The TTC — every bus and subway in Toronto — stopped dead. Traffic tangled and snarled in minutes. We could have evacuated a lot of healthy people. Our job wasn't to serve and protect, though. The task was *containment*.

Whoever was in charge didn't want commuters to get to the GO trains. They couldn't allow millions of people pouring out of Toronto to the suburbs, out to Oakville and up to Barrie. Housing was so expensive, some even commuted from an hour or two away. Whatever happened next, the powers that be were trying to keep the disaster from going global. If we failed to contain the threat, they needed the maximum population concentration at the city center. They were prepping for a bomb drop if it was needed. I used to think people like that were cold monsters with ice for hearts. With time, I've come to believe they were not bad, just fearful. If you asked any one of them, they'd say no terrible things were done that day. When they did terrible things, or ordered others to do the unspeakable, they called it the *responsible* thing.

I was supposed to keep the situation in hand. I am guilty of doing the responsible thing. I'm so sorry. When I was a kid, fear was the last thing any boy was supposed to admit to. Lately, I've gathered a greater appreciation of fear. I understand it now that I feel it all the time.

Staff Sergeant Barnes led the way toward the entrance to the Box, shield up. "Safeties off. We may be dealing with terrorists. Assume nothing and let me do the thinking. Understood, squad?"

"Ready to rock," we chorused.

We passed the body of the dead woman. Face down on the concrete steps, what had once been the back of her head was now a messy hole.

Lundsden slowed to look. "She was wounded — "

"You'll make detective one day," Davis crowed.

"Before Crenshaw took the shot, I mean."

"The Staff Sergeant said to let him do the thinking, Lundsden."

Barnes didn't have to weigh in. Mac's command came in louder than necessary over our headphones. "Do not touch that body or you'll end up in a quarantine tent for a month."

Davis gave Lundsden a nudge and we moved on, letting Staff Sergeant Barnes set the pace.

I glanced back at Lundsden. His gaze was on the ground. His head was not in the game. The bomb tech was a valuable team member but I suspected he wasn't suited to this task. I might have saved him then if I could have spoken with the Staff Sergeant privately. I should have told him to send Lundsden back to Mac. I spared the man's feelings instead of sparing his life.

Barnes paused, his weapon trained on the entrance. He could have keyed his throat mike but his words were for the squad only. "Nobody comes out. If anybody gets past you, everybody's dead. Understand? We go in and reconnoiter, slow and cautious."

In reply, we sounded off:

"Two, go," I said.

"Three, understood." Lundsden's voice shook.

"Four, copy," Taylor said.

"Five, roger that." Davis sounded as relaxed as if we were off to visit the little zoo in High Park. *Poser.*

Our breath betrayed us. Our nervous systems were nervous and our breaths came too fast. Even with the summer heatwave bearing down on us and carrying thirty-two pounds of gear each, our breath was rapid and shallow. I took a deeper breath and let it out, long and slow between my clenched teeth as I tapped my O2 meter. Without comment, the others picked up on my cue and consciously slowed their breathing, too. It wouldn't do to let our audience see us collapse to the pavement from hyperventilation before we got inside.

I looked back toward the bank. Across the narrow street, a pretty woman watched us from behind the glass by the ATM. Her gaze seemed fixed on the fallen woman on the steps. Many faces pressed to those windows bore witness, but that tall striking woman in a white summer dress caught my eye most. Long red ringlets hung past her shoulders. She had a long, angular nose and full ruby lips. Her large eyes would make her stand out in any crowd. She also looked the most terrified.

Don't worry, pretty lady, I thought. *We'll keep the danger bottled up so you'll be home safe tonight.*

We didn't need the battering ram on Lundsden's back. Someone as large as a football player must have barreled through the front door to Echidna Biosystems. The door had been pushed so far back, the mechanism that closed it automatically was broken. The doorway to Hell yawned open in the hot breeze, welcoming us.

"Two, recon the lobby." The Staff Sergeant's voice was muffled behind his mask. Frank Barnes sounded like a haunted man.

I peered into the lobby. It looked like any other office building except for the metal detectors and two security desks instead of one. Both stood empty. I guessed that when an alarm goes off on Level 4, a private security guard making minimum wage plus overtime isn't going to stick his neck out too far. Come to think of it, the effort to save the world wasn't worth my pay grade and OT, either.

Besides a few pieces of paper on the floor that had spilled from a briefcase on the conveyor belt at the security chokepoint, there was nothing much to see. Two pairs of high heeled shoes lay orphaned on the lobby floor. Apparently, some staff ran as soon as the alarm began blaring. How many really knew all that was going on down in Level 4? Did they understand the mischief the virologists were up to? Even if they did know, a job is a job. They probably still would have worked there. The World Trade Center was a target long before 9/11. Still, thousands went to work every day until a known terrorist target became Ground Zero. We work on automatic. We operate under the blind expectation that we'll be safe.

I signaled to the Staff Sergeant that I had no news for him and he nodded. "Two by two, go."

We stepped into the lobby. The alarm was much louder than I thought. It sounded like a submarine klaxon from an old movie. It jangled my nerves and made verbal communication almost impossible. Why the hell does anyone make a siren so loud that it rumbles your eardrums and sends vibrations through your chest? The intent is to alert everyone to the danger. Instead, it's difficult to hear orders, helpful warnings or a pack of killer maniacs infected with something deadly designed to kill us all.

5

A s I got deeper into the lobby, I saw the genius of the building's design. The office tower stopped at the mezzanine level above us. The skyscraper's elevators didn't go up from this lobby, only down. Somewhere above us, office workers were being ushered from their cubicles and taking the stairs. When they exited the building, they'd spill out onto Dundas a block north of the entrance to Echidna Biosystems.

Only our Staff Sergeants had trained for this task. If the powers that be had more forethought, everyone on the team would know the layout and what to expect. At the time I assumed this was some kind of oversight on Mac's part. Later, I figured out that keeping us ignorant was part of the plan.

Barnes led the way, and as soon as he crossed the threshold of the metal detector, it lit up like a Christmas tree and let out a series of loud chirps. We all froze for a moment and a grim chuckle, as cold as a death rattle, spread through the squad. It was a battlefield reaction, two parts silly and one part serious.

Barnes glanced my way and I caught his annoyed look through his hood's face shield. He waved us forward. I leaned over the counter and turned off the gateway's metal detector. One deafening klaxon was enough.

Silver elevator doors faced us, gleaming and locked. The down button flashed red. As soon as the alarm sounded, a series of automated protocols shut down the elevators. I wondered if anyone might have been trapped in one or both of those elevators when the alarm sounded. The alarms would tell them the end of the world had arrived, but what then? The long wait.

In movies, if you find yourself trapped in an elevator, you can call for help using the phone in the control panel. Modern elevators have an escape hatch but it can only be opened from the outside. Some smart risk assessment lawyer came up with the bright observation that nobody wants a panicky passenger losing his or her shit and crawling up into the shaft before a maintenance worker can come and free them. That knowledge wouldn't be much solace if you were trapped in that elevator in the Box. With the alarms going and the rest of staff running for their lives, you could scream yourself hoarse before you figured out you'd been left behind. No one would starve to death in there. The lack of water would kill them first. Too slowly, the prison would become a tomb.

I looked around the corner to the left. At first glance, I thought I was looking at a gleaming white hallway, but it was not straight. It was a long white ramp that stretched out a couple hundred feet before it began to spiral to the right and angle down. Aside from the alarm, there were no signs of trouble. No bodies littered the shiny floor.

If this were a movie, there'd be a bloody smeared handprint down the wall. That was to come and I'd be the one making that bloody smear.

The Staff Sergeant signaled to me to cover him. It was tempting to move fast but Frank Barnes was an experienced officer. He took his time rather than rushing into the unknown. As I sidestepped to the opposite wall, I felt exposed now that I was out from behind his ballistic shield. The ramp curved sharply so I needed to sacrifice my position to get the better angle on the shooting solution. It is bad form to shoot a fellow officer in the back. Soon, that wouldn't seem like such a bad idea.

At the bottom of the ramp, we came to our first body inside the Box.

6

The corpse blocked the door to Level 1. She lay face down, a large middle-aged woman in a dress the color of mustard. Her blood was the usual ketchup red. No plague got this one. She'd been trampled. Barnes pushed the corpse with the toe of his boot. Her eyes were open, staring into the dark forever, scouting ahead to find the way, to discover what happens after Hell erupts on Earth.

One by one, we stepped over the corpse into a small cubicle farm. Lundsden, the last in, bent beside the body. The hem of the woman's dress was ripped and her bottom was exposed. Her underwear was a pretty floral print stained with shit and blood. Using the muzzle of his weapon, the bomb tech pulled the hem of the dress down, covering the woman's bum and thighs.

"Head in the game, Noob," Davis chided.

Lundsden straightened a little faster than dignity allowed and shouldered his MP5 again. I didn't know what I was getting into then. I should have known Lundsden wasn't long for this world. The new world is an unforgiving place. Dying times don't allow for niceties.

The tidy office was lit with bright fluorescents. We could have been in any office building. Taylor, the squad's weapons tech, joined me in checking under a line of desks. No one was hiding there. I expected horrors like in the movies, maybe a damsel in distress, a cowardly bureaucrat or a corpse melting into the Berber carpet. None of the above.

I keyed my throat mike. "Nada, sir."

Barnes nodded and toggled his radio to inform Mac. "Level 1 employees bugged out. Judging by the empty desks, you might be looking for a dozen people, plus a security guard or two up top. Request we check with the security company. The emblem at the front desk said the security company was Maple." He spelled it. "Maple Security Initiatives was the contractor. Over."

"We're working on getting names and last known addresses," Mac replied. "We're working with Ottawa to get a list of employees. The last report we have puts the number of employees on Level 1 at fifteen. The date on the report is three years old, though. Over."

"We've got one dead, a female, at the top of Level 1. Looks like she was trampled. Over."

"We've got more than one DB," Lundsden said. He beckoned Barnes toward a door. "A security guard."

I moved around a line of desks to peer past the Staff Sergeant. The door led to a room that was barely bigger than a walk-in closet. An array of wires led to a modem. The slim panel of furiously blinking lights seemed like an odd electronic echo of life in the dead office. Below the modem I could see a photocopier, shelves of paper, a broom and two legs splayed out on the floor. The pants had stripes up the legs.

"Dead as shit," Barnes announced. "Movin' on."

As the Staff Sergeant backed out, Lundsden followed him so I got a better view. I wished I hadn't looked. A bald man in his mid-fifties wore a shirt that had once been white. Now it was spattered red and gray. A pistol lay in his lap and a gaping hole dripped blood where his left temple should have been.

Davis stuck his head in front of me for a quick glance. "Suicide."

"No way," Lundsden said. "That's murder."

Davis didn't care to be corrected. "How many suicides have you seen? That's what they look like, kid."

"Suicides don't usually drop the gun," Lundsden replied. "The angle is all wrong. The entry point is a touch too far back for the bullet to exit the skull that far forward. And most of all, who kills themselves at work next to the photocopier in a closet?"

"Suicides are either depressed, scared, stupid or fed up." Davis looked around. "That alarm would scare anyone stupid. Anybody see a way to turn it off?"

We were in the dark but Barnes knew how the Box worked. "Once the alarm goes off, the only way to shut it off is to get to the control room on Level 3. There are two locks to go through to get there. Stop playing *Murder, She Wrote* and can the chatter. Finish checking this level quick. The guard's nametag says his name was Tarique. No last name. Lundsden, call it in to Mac."

We call guys who talk too much "oxygen thieves." That thought was never more appropriate. We'd already lost too much time to the Box.

7

I spotted a small picture frame on a desk. Everything can go to shit in the time it takes to glance the wrong way.

When I was in high school, I remember walking down the hallway from history class with a textbook over my crotch. I had a rager of an erection. At sixteen, such afflictions often appear with little to no provocation. My face burning with embarrassment and sweat beading on my forehead, I made my way through a crowded corridor. If I dropped my books, I wouldn't have been able to pick them up. If any of these girls looks too closely, I'd be known for the rest of my life as the freak walking through the school with a hard-on. And if any of my buddies found out, they'd laugh and never let me forget it. For that humiliation, I would have begged my parents to let me change schools.

I got through my high school ordeal undetected, but my point is, *everything* is exactly that tenuous. For instance, I wish to God now that I hadn't seen that picture on the desk. It was the tall girl I had assumed worked for the bank, the one with the ringlets. In the picture, her ginger hair was shorter and straight. There was no denying those large eyes, though. The snap was taken at a beach. She stood in gentle surf up to mid-thigh wearing a blue tankini that made her hair look even more red. A handsome, heavily muscled guy with a wide smile stood beside her. Their arms wrapped around each other. She wore a big rock of an engagement ring. That happy couple looked like they would live forever. If I were him, I'd smile, too.

The worst part? I was working on automatic. I wasn't thinking about ramifications and consequences. My defense is common and equally amoral: "I was just doing my job."

I keyed my mic. "Two to Ops, be advised, an employee from Echidna is at the bank. Tall woman, red hair, white dress. I spotted her in the atrium by the ATM." I opened her desk drawers looking for a name. Pencils, paper clips, assorted notes and files. I saw no business cards but she had used a label maker to clearly print out her computer password. Idiotic, but understandable. Since system administrators had begun insisting passwords be renewed and different every three months, everybody started writing down their passwords and keeping them handy.

I pushed the space bar on the computer and the dark screen brightened to a login page. I didn't need a password. The screen read: *Make it a great day, Kaela!*

"Is that all, Two? Over." Mac asked.

"First name, Kaela, K-A-E-L-A. No last name evident ... " Then, at the back of a drawer, I spotted an envelope addressed to her. "Hold. I got it. Last name: Santini. S-A-N-T-I-N-I. Over."

"Roger that. We'll cross-check the employee list and interview her. Over."

Frank added in, "She's got a desk on Level 1, Mac. She's probably only support staff from Level 1. Over."

Mac clicked his mic twice as shorthand for, "I got it," and there was no more from the radio. He must have been busy rounding up the onlookers to figure out who they all were.

Women like a man in uniform. That's what got me into this mess. I was glad to be on an elite team of professionals who saved lives — ordinarily our job was to *save* lives. The ETF started as an ad hoc force called out for extraordinary circumstances. That wasn't the job anymore. We broke down doors every day. When there wasn't enough of that to do, we ran drills to see how fast we could breach a plane in a hangar at Toronto International. We fired hundreds of rounds a week to stay sharp. We exercised to keep ourselves fit for the demands of duty we hoped would never come. My point is, when the regular force needed us, we were the cavalry. I miss that feeling.

I found out later that, as we checked Level 1, another team was gathering in the street. We were the probe. The JTF-2 team outside was supposed to be the solution. Joint Task Force 2 saw us as part of the problem.

It never occurred to me that I wasn't one of the good guys. I used to be so proud of this uniform.

EPISODE 2

zombie (noun)

1. A person suffering existential angst or rage and trapped in banality, characterized by despair at interminable suboptimal life conditions and boredom, possibly escalating to violence or self-harm.

2. A ravenous cannibal, usually, though not necessarily, dead; a revenant defying death who hunts for the living to kill and feed or to convert victims to his or her kind. Origin: Voodoo religion; popularized in fiction.

3. A person carrying the Class I or Class II Picasso agent. (See also: AFTER)

~ Notes from NEXT

8

The entrance to Level 2 was secured by a gate with heavy steel doors. Wire reinforced the slab of thick glass. The door's lock consisted of a heavy industrial alphanumeric keypad. I'd seen similar pads but never one built to withstand a sledge hammer blow.

"What do you see?" Barnes asked me above the din of the klaxon.

"Set up like an airlock, sir."

"Technically, it's called a decontamination chamber. We go in. With the lockdown alarm going, nobody below us can get out, not without the code." The Staff Sergeant leaned his shield against the steel door but kept his MP5 at the ready. He stepped to the keypad and pulled a lanyard from a Velcro pocket. From a laminated yellow card, he scanned a series of numbers and letters. With his left hand, Barnes keyed in: 5 - 5 - A - Z - 2 - 5 - 0 - 0 - L - 1 - 1 - V - 3 - T - P - D - Q. He tried the code twice. The lock buzzed each time but failed to click open. Slowly, he tried the sequence one more time with the same result.

"Did the silly buggers change the code?" Davis asked. "They haven't kept their staffing list up to date."

Barnes shook his head. "Couldn't change it. Nobody on this site has the code to get out after lockdown. This is the master override code. When the sensors detect some breach, the alarm goes off and everything shuts down automagically, nobody in or out. To move between the levels, we have to enter the code and crank the hatches by hand. Anything happens to me … " He waved the card at us. "Everybody got it?"

As one person, the squad said, "Yessir!"

"Then why isn't the code working, Frank?" Davis asked.

"Maybe they keep the germs out but my fingers are too fat in these damn gloves." To our horror, Barnes pulled at the duct tape around his wrist to remove his outer glove. The outer latex glove came with it so he was down to one thin layer of latex. Frank keyed in the code. The lock clicked open with one long buzz and I spun the lever to yank the door open.

Only when he turned around did the Staff Sergeant see us staring at his hand. "Don't worry, boys! Still pretty safe. When we get out I'll sterilize it with Purell and steam it for an hour. If that doesn't work, we can cut it off, burn it and bury the ashes. Big trouble for my sex life, though."

Chuckling nervously, all five of us pushed into the decontamination chamber. The heavy steel door closed behind us and high powered fans blew some kind of yellow dust onto our suits. The chamber was bigger than I expected, built not just for people but to get equipment in and out. Still, I thought of curses on tombs in sealed pyramids and a frisson of claustrophobia made me tighten my jaw as my anxiety rose another notch.

Taylor wondered aloud what was in the air blasting around us. I told him it was the latest fragrance from Paris. "It's called Apocalypse."

"Shut up, Harmon," Barnes said. "It's my mission. I'm the only one allowed to make jokes."

"No jokes at all, sir?"

"I'll let you know."

"Yes, sir, thank you, sir."

As the air cycled through the chamber, my ears popped. The others must have felt it, too. We got more fidgety.

"Should it take this long?" Davis asked.

"It takes as long as it takes," Barnes said. "It takes a little longer in the next part. This gets us to the staging area. Level 3 is the lab. Level 4 is the virus vault."

"Permission to have a brain, sir?" I asked.

"Until that far door opens, we can pretend, sure," he replied.

"But if that woman on the front step was infected with something — "

"I don't think she was infected," Lundsden put in. "She was hurt but I don't think she was sick."

"Stop that train of thought, Lundsden," Davis said. "There will be plenty of time for Monday morning quarterbacking on Monday morning."

Barnes didn't seem to mind Davis shutting Lundsden down. "Simple answer to your question, Harmon. The woman currently polluting our street by inconsiderately bleeding all over the place was probably the source of the containment breach. We don't know what we're dealing with or how long the sickness takes before it's communicable and in full effect. Remember my rules."

We did remember. Mac was a by the book sort of cop but Frank Barnes had rules of engagement nobody wrote down. Our leader had five rules. Usually he was in some high perch on overwatch scoping out a hostage taker through a window. To keep us sharp when a call became drawn out and the waiting got heavy, Frank would occasionally recite his theories of police work:

1. Bad guys are stupid. Be smarter than the bad guys.

2. There's no crying unless Frank cries and Frank don't cry.

3. Don't take your work home with you. No unhappy spouses, no drinking to excess ... or at least not because of the job.

4. Everybody goes home at the end of the shift. Death of a suspect was to be avoided when possible because of the extra paper-work it would entail. Death of a fellow officer was to be avoided because police funerals in Toronto require bagpipes. Frank hates bagpipes.

5. When one of us shoots at a suspect, we all shoot. In the expenditure of bullets, we were to spare no expense. If called upon to kill, no waiting. Details are things to sort out later.

The air finished cycling and the chem sprayers stopped. "Playtime is over, gentlemen. Follow my lead."

We pushed forward through the blowers and entered Level 2. Looking around, I wondered what this area smelled like. With my respirator plastered uncomfortably tight to my face, I had no idea. It looked like it might have that strong aroma hospitals have: industrial cleaner atop a sterile hint of mortality.

I was beginning to sweat more heavily under my hood and mask. The palms of my thick gloves were rubber so my hands wouldn't slip on my weapon. That wouldn't be much help if the lenses on my mask fogged. My hands and head felt hot but my feet were cold. I felt clumsy. Adrenaline had pushed my heart rate too high. I consciously slowed my respiration again. Lundsden picked up on what I was doing and mirrored my inhalations and exhalations. When you can't control anything else, all you can do is get hold of your breathing and wait.

I was slightly relieved to find that Level 2 appeared to be abandoned. Ghost towns crossed my mind, though. Look at any old map and compare it to a new map. You'll find places that don't exist anymore. Towns get abandoned, sometimes inexplicably. Any old village churchyard tells grim stories. Do a rubbing over barely legible gravestones and you'll find waves of deaths as influenza took all the babies, children and old people. Sometimes more than that. Little towns die. People flee burning cities.

I wondered if someday someone will look at an old map, compare it to a new map, and ask, "Anybody ever hear of a place called, 'Toronto?'"

9

Taylor shouted. "I got a DB here!"

"Coming, Steve," I replied. This level was as wide as a large house. It didn't take long for me to find Taylor near the end of a long narrow shower room, The staging area appeared to split into showers and a locker room. Empty biohazard suits hung open like deflated balloons, or maybe like dejected ghosts.

As Lundsden and I rushed to Taylor, Barnes chastised him for raising his voice. "It's a radio. You don't have to shout. You're killing my ear, dumbass."

Taylor apologized without looking up from the corpse. He stood at the curtain to a stall. It could have been a changeroom at any clothing store. The floor angled down slightly to a depression in the center of the shower area so tentacles of blood reached for the drain.

Taylor used the barrel of his weapon to pull back the curtain so Lundsden and I could take a look. The corpse was a naked man in his late thirties or early forties. He had a few gray hairs in his beard. He'd never have to worry about going grayer. Blood trickled from his mouth but it had gushed from a gaping wound that stretched from his navel down into his ruined groin. It was all a red mash.

"What virus does that?" Lundsden asked.

"Split from asshole to appetite," Taylor said absently.

Barnes didn't bother to show up. He keyed his throat mic instead. "Not interested in the dead ones, boys. Let's find some live ones. Report to the next lock to go to the lab."

I suspect we were all relieved to do as ordered.

"Maybe the rest got out," Taylor suggested.

"They didn't," Barnes said. "Levels 2, 3 and 4 go into lockdown after the contagion alarm goes off. There's no time to get out once the outbreak alarm sounds. They've only got a few seconds. I'm sure there are people trapped below."

"A few seconds, though? Why not simultaneously, sir?" Lundsden asked.

"Because you don't want those heavy doors slamming shut and cutting a lab tech in half," Barnes told him. "Blood, guts and bone might mess up the hermetic seals on the doors, don't you think?"

"Then why are we down here breaching these seals at all? Why not quarantine everybody who's trapped where they are, set up communication and figure it out from there?"

It was a decent question. When Chernobyl went up and spewed radiation across Europe, the government evacuated the people and told them never to go back. The Staff Sergeant's only answer was, "Orders."

There were reasons why we were sent in — not good ones, but reasons. There was something down in the Box that was valuable and somebody in a position to give orders wanted it. Maybe they wanted to reuse this facility. Maybe we had to secure the lab so nobody else could get out ... or in. Maybe the plan was to get hold of something before medical professionals who knew what they were looking at got down here.

I could have become a physiotherapist but my college girlfriend said I would look good in a cop's uniform. If she hadn't said that, I probably wouldn't be where I am now. That girlfriend cheated on me with a buddy from the basketball team in our senior year. They both moved to New York State. She's working in a dentist's office while he studies to become a chiropractor.

We do all sorts of crazy things for silly reasons. I saw people do stupid things every day in my work. Worse, we fall into things and come up with the rationale for our actions after the fact. I didn't think I made silly mistakes. I assumed everyone else was an idiot. But here I was, proceeding to Level 3.

I've had a lot of time to think since we went down into the Box. Having time to think is not always as good as it sounds.

10

Somebody pounded on the decontamination chamber door. Between the thickness of the door and the alarm sounding, we wouldn't have heard it if they used their fists. They smacked the door with something metal.

Barnes put a hand on the door and waited. "Dit-dit-dit, dah-dah-dah, dit-dit-dit."

"S.O.S." Lundsden declared the obvious.

Davis told him to shut up. Taylor cursed. I said nothing.

Barnes ordered Davis to close the hatch to Level 2 behind us. He did as he was told and, after a short buzz, shower nozzles blasted us with water as a red light glowed above the far door. There was surely more than water in the spray but nobody told me what chemicals we might be exposing ourselves to. Our environmental suits were supposed to protect us but they weren't quite as bulky and shapeless as a normal biohazard suit, either. We had gear on our belts and backs that did not lend itself to easy sterilization protocols.

The Staff Sergeant pulled open a small access door on the wall, apparently familiar with the controls. I thought again how we should have all been better prepared. We ran hostage scenarios at the airport three times a year. Why not have an ETF field trip into the Box when the alarms *weren't* blaring?

"I'm getting a mother of a headache," Davis said. "We gotta shut off that damn alarm."

"From the control room. Almost there." Barnes pushed a button and a screen revealed the view from a camera on the other side of the steel door. The person sending the plea for help wore a bulky biohazard suit. He or she was using the leg of a metal chair to pound on the door.

I keyed my throat mic. "Two to Ops. We have visual on a survivor, at the door to the exit of Level 3. Over."

No reply came.

"The radio won't work now that we're entering 3," Barnes said. "No cell phones, either. That's why we don't have the relatives of the employees screaming at the barricades."

As we waited to get deeper into the Box, families of these employees were still going about their day, oblivious to the danger to their loved ones. I wondered how long this breach could remain a secret and what would happen when word got out?

I tapped the oxygen indicator on my wrist. "Let's get in and out so we report to Mac in person. This place creeps me out."

As the chamber's gear finished its cycle, the water nozzles sprayed us with an orange chemical mist that gathered in thick beads. The slime rolled down our gear as quick as mercury. Finally, a blue UV light surrounded us as scanners hummed somewhere behind the wall.

Through it all, the pounding on the far door continued, a staccato metronome communicating desperation.

I stood beside the Staff Sergeant as he stared at the figure on the security cam screen. I was probably the only person who heard him. "No communication back to Earth. We're alone. We may as well be on the moon. We're moon men now. Earth rules do not apply here." Barnes might have been talking to himself.

I was already nervous. Not that panic ever helps but, when my superior officer started talking to himself, I should have picked up on the clue to freak out.

11

A buzzer sounded as the door to Level 3 opened. The figure in the bulky biohazard suit stepped back, still holding an office chair. "Took you long enough!"

Through her faceplate, I could see the woman's dirty blonde hair plastered across her forehead. She was sweating hard and I wondered if it was fear or the effort of pounding on the door. Or was it fever? I prayed it wasn't fever. Barnes had his shield and MP5 up and in position to do business so we all pointed our weapons at her.

"What's with the guns?"

"Identify yourself!" Barnes demanded.

"Dr. Christine Newberry. If you point your damn guns somewhere else, you can call me Chris."

The Staff Sergeant didn't exactly take his weapon off her but he let the barrel point down a couple inches. "What happened?"

"I don't know. I was about to go back to the control room when the alarm went off. Someone messed up big time."

"Okay, Chris. How many people are working today?"

"It's a skeleton crew. Three of my colleagues are at a conference. It's the first week of July, so a bunch of people are off to Cottage

Country. Between the Canada Day long weekend, the conference for the bigwigs in Aruba and summer holidays — "

"How many on Level 1?" Barnes said a little louder.

"I don't know. The people up top are support staff. I don't really know them well at all. I certainly don't know their vacation schedules. I spend all my time down here." She paused to think. "There might be … I dunno … nine, maybe? It could be twelve."

I had a grease pencil tucked into a compartment on my sleeve at my left shoulder. I took it out and wrote, *12* on the vinyl shell of my environmental suit. Adding up the guard under the blinking modem, the trampled woman, Kaela and the dead woman on the front steps, I added: 4. *+, -, ?*

"Twelve on Level 1?" Barnes echoed. "Okay, it seems they got out."

"That's not the protocol. They're supposed to stay put. Nobody stayed up top?"

Barnes ignored her question. "How many on Level 4?"

"Four. Two docs in the vault's lab and two techs running experiments in the Box. I think … "

"You're not sure?" Davis said.

The doctor pursed her lips. "I don't know, man! Every time we want to take a leak we have to go up to Level 2, shower and go through the whole isolation protocol again. People come up and down a lot."

"Great system." I could hear the sarcasm drip through Patrick's tone. "You guys got complacent."

"With that damn alarm going, my nerves are all jangly. Let's get out of here!"

"Everybody stays until we get this sorted out. How do we know you're not a terrorist?"

"Davis!" Barnes barked. "De-escalate."

"Yes, sir." He nodded and stepped back but Patrick Davis's voice told me he was already far away, probably thinking about crawling into his bed at home. That's what I was doing.

I'd seen Davis under stress before but this felt different. It was as if we were used to exploring caves but now we were doing the same task far underwater and encumbered by SCUBA gear we hated. I sympathized. Sweat slipped down my forehead and salt burned my eyes. My nose was itchy again but there was nothing I could do about it.

He was right, too. The lab had become complacent if they allowed employees to come and go without tracking where everyone was. I imagined no one on the International Space Station was ever so easygoing about safety protocols.

"I'm no terrorist," the doctor said. "This has got to be some kind of system failure."

Lundsden surprised me by taking the initiative after the Staff Sergeant told Davis to shut his gob. "Got anything special downstairs, Dr. Newberry?"

"There's always something special down there. The vault contains four freezer pods that hold some of the world's most deadly bugs. We've got various killer strains of the popular scary things. The latest additions are frozen tissue samples from a failed Arctic expedition from the early 1900s. We're figuring out what a team of British explorers died of."

"But you think there are typically four people working on Level 4?" Barnes pressed.

"Likely. There are only three air hoses for three suits in the main work area, max. Two are for work and one for emergencies in case anyone needs to be dragged out. You don't want a bunch of people tripping over each other down there."

"What do you think triggered the alarm?"

"I don't know. Maybe one of techs on 4 pulled the alarm or there's some kind of equipment failure that set it off. A change in air pressure could trip the sensors. Each floor from 2 down has neg air pressure — "

"To keep the germs in, not out," Barnes said.

Newberry waved her gloved hand vaguely to a door behind her. "I've got six lab techs on this level. They aren't feeling well. Could be nerves, though."

"Why do you say that?" I asked.

"I feel fine," she said. "They didn't look sick until the alarm started blaring. The power of suggestion is strong. You see somebody throw up, you want to puke, too, so — "

Barnes spoke in a calm, soothing voice I'd only heard him use on hostage takers. "Chris, listen carefully. We've got bodies on 1 and 2. This is not the power of suggestion, a drill or a mistake. Something serious is happening here."

"Oh."

I could barely hear her small voice. She was so used to dealing with deadly viruses that it never occurred to her they'd turn on her one day. I went out on a call to a little house in Scarborough once. A guy kept tigers in his basement. He made the same mistake.

Side note: Don't keep tigers in your basement, but if you do, make sure they are well fed. If you don't make a lot of burgers for a predator, they'll make a burger out of you.

This bit of wisdom became important later, too.

"What were you working on today?" Barnes asked the doctor.

"Mostly? Madagascar has an outbreak of bubonic plague. It might be mutating and we're trying to figure out if there's a new vector. We've all got different projects, though."

I'd read about the Madagascar outbreak on Facebook a couple of times in the past week. Death and mayhem on the other side of the world had seemed so remote and irrelevant, it may as well have been happening on another planet. I'd become much more interested in frightening diseases in the last — I glanced at the oxygen meter on my wrist — eighteen minutes. Could it have been that long already? Between coming in too slow, moving around too fast, speaking and waiting, I suspected we'd been using more air than we should have. If we'd prepared better, been given time to run through a few practice runs …

I pushed the thought away, waved to get the Staff Sergeant's attention and tapped my wrist to urge him to move his interview process along.

He nodded and asked, "Chris, who's in the control room now?"

"I was in there but one of the techs — Cherry Gillis — called me to the lab."

"Which lab?" Barnes sounded patient, like he had all the time in the world.

She pointed vaguely at the double doors leading to the laboratory on the same level. "This one, down the hall."

"You left your post," Davis said.

She looked at him evenly and some steel came into her voice. "This is an office, not a military installation. I'm a doctor, not a soldier."

"I understand what you're saying." Barnes's reply betrayed no hint of irritation at Davis or his interview subject. He seemed to show no emotion at all, in fact. "What did this Cherry Gillis have to say?"

"We spoke about her symptoms — just a headache, no big deal. I was on my way back when the alarm went off. I need to get in there to see what's happening and to shut off this alarm! Can we please shut off the alarm? My entry code won't work!"

"Who is on Level 4?"

"Dr. Hamish Allen — he's the senior staffer on site most of the time. Also, Dr. Natalie Gignac and two lab techs, Glen and Arthur. That's who should be there, I think."

"Should be? You think?"

"They might have been on Level 2 or maybe they even went out to get a Starbucks or a Timmy's. I was up all night working and busy this morning. The senior staff have keycards so they come and go. I can't watch the surveillance cameras every minute. I've been catching up on filing before taking off on vacation. I'm not even supposed to be here today!"

Barnes shrugged. "I guess that's fine as long as everyone stays where they are. We can get into the control room to confirm who's where and then everything will be fine — "

"You can? Great! The bigwigs who have the emergency code are all at the Aruba conference. I can't call them because of the damn security protocols! The lockdown is supposed to be for our protection but so far it's screwing me up, y'know?"

"Brilliant," Davis said. "How can you people screw around with microscopes and still — "

"Don't look at me," she said. "Master codes are above my pay grade, high security and all that bullshit. I only started here in May. They don't trust me to get the Friday afternoon pizza orders right for the weekly staff meeting."

"Fine. Are the sick lab techs locked in the lab?" Barnes asked.

She nodded. "Yeah. I talked to them on the intercom a few minutes ago. If I hadn't been headed back to the control room when the lockdown happened, I'd be stuck in the Level 3 lab, too. They're in the conference room, actually. We might need an evacuation team of virologists who are used to handling hazardous materials. Or maybe all we really need is an HVAC tech who can reinstall freon in a freezer pod. If this is a simple sensor getting a false read on temperature in the vault or something, I'm going to be so pissed!"

"Thank you, Chris," the Staff Sergeant said. "Please lead the way to the control room."

She pointed to her left. The large steel door was less than ten feet away. The steel alphanumeric keypad, almost identical to the apparatus on Level 1, gleamed next to the door. The only difference was this one had a slot to swipe a keycard, as well. "The control room is right there. Get me in, quick!"

"Lead the way, Chris."

"No offense, glad you're here and all, but we don't need guys with guns. I need the door code." She beckoned us forward.

"We're here to provide security, Ma'am," Taylor said. The way he said it, I had an inkling that, when all this was over, he might ask Christine Newberry for her number. Among the youngest guys in the ETF, Steve had the reputation for being the biggest hound.

She turned and took a couple of steps. "Security? Look at all these steel doors! I feel safe enough, thanks."

"We don't provide security for you, Chris," the Staff Sergeant said. "We're here for everybody else's safety." Barnes shot her in the back of the head once at close range.

Dr. Christine Newberry flopped to the floor. The Staff Sergeant shot her twice more in the chest, dead center.

Barnes stepped back, careful to avoid the pool of blood spreading from the body. "You're wrong, kid. This *is* a military installation and you *were* a soldier."

That's what the Staff Sergeant meant when he said he would "do the interviewing."

13

W e all froze. We weren't supposed to freeze but it seemed all we could do was stare at the murdered woman. Barnes turned to regard each of us. "This is what securing the location looks like. We have to assume they're all infected. We erase the threat."

"Whether it's a threat or not?" Lundsden asked. He seemed to recover first and grasp the situation faster than the rest of us. "It's a hard reboot, then. 'Securing the location' sure looks like murder, doesn't it?"

"Shut up, Bobby!" Davis barked.

Taylor wasn't looking at the doctor's corpse. Steve was looking at me, *to* me. We'd gone fishing together. He was the only team member I knew well outside the job. He was waiting for me to say something but my throat had gone dry and I said nothing. Until that moment, I hadn't done much I should be ashamed of.

"Hold up. It makes sense," Davis said. "It would be worse if we didn't already have bodies upstairs. The contamination could get out of control. We're here to nip an epidemic in the bud."

"By killing doctors," Lundsden said. "I sure hope it's not what she said, a faulty sensor on a freezer."

Barnes raised his weapon and pointed it at Lundsden. I pointed my MP5 at the Staff Sergeant so Taylor did the same. Davis — who never heard an order he didn't like — pointed his submachine gun at me. The bomb tech just stood there pretending he was Switzerland.

"Everybody be cool," Barnes said. "You guys don't have to understand the order. I'll do that for you. My mission, my responsibility."

"What are we supposed to say at the inquiry?" I asked. "Am I supposed to tell some tribunal that I was only following orders? That woman wasn't even sick."

"You don't know she wasn't," he replied. "We don't know how long it takes for the bug to take over."

Take over. That seemed like an odd way to put it. I later found out that was the perfect way to put it.

"Here's what happened: An infected person met us at the front door. In a lab like this, if a bug gets out, somebody's got to go in and shut that shit down. Doing the hard stuff is what somebodies do. This is the job. You can philosophize and whine about it later but keep it to yourself around me. There isn't going to be an inquiry, Harmon. We do our job and this time next week maybe they salvage the lab. Maybe they pour concrete down here until it's a solid block. That's not our business. Now everybody stand down. *Everybody.*"

Barnes pointed his weapon at the floor first. Davis was still drawn down on me and didn't look like he wanted to ease off. The Staff Sergeant gestured for him to lower his weapon and Davis relented. Taylor and I followed suit.

"We've got bodies upstairs," Davis said. "This place is already compromised."

"Are you trying to convince us or yourself?" Lundsden asked.

"Shut it!"

"Bob's right," I said. "Glad you don't have a weapon on me anymore. Your finger shouldn't be on a trigger right now. You look shaky, Patrick."

"I can do my damn job. Can you? And I'm not shaky ... not

because … " He pointed at the dead doctor. "I'm freaking because I don't want to get sick. Viruses and shit? You heard what she said about what they keep down here. Let's do the job and get out. I don't know about you, Harmon, but I don't want to die of plague. The plague? Jesus! They mess with that stuff, they get what they get. A bullet is a mercy compared to shitting yourself to death."

"Easy, guys," Barnes said. "If we all do our jobs and watch each other's backs, we'll all get out of here quick. Everybody take a deep breath."

I tapped my wrist meaningfully. I was twenty-four minutes into my oxygen supply.

Barnes nodded his acknowledgment. "On second thought, suck it up, buttercups. Clear this place. It shouldn't take long. We get out and we get a long vacation after this. Isolation, hazard pay and pretty nurses."

"Yeah, we'll need quite some time to tell ourselves this was all okay," Lundsden said.

The Staff Sergeant waved his objection away. "The people who sent us had lots of time to think about the right and the wrong of it. It's not up to you because it's not supposed to be. You can't make clean decisions while you're in the shit. That's why this contingency was planned ahead of time by people who are not in said shit. What we do today saves lives, lots of them. Clear, Lundsden?"

"Clear,"

"Taylor?"

"Y-yes, sir. Clear."

"Harmon?"

"Yes … sir."

Barnes didn't even bother to ask Davis. In his whole life, Patrick never considered that he might be wrong about anything.

And so our fates were sealed. It's really easy to commit to do something stupid.

"Everything's going to be peachy!" Barnes said.

The alarm stopped so abruptly that when the Staff Sergeant said, "Going to be peachy," he was still shouting above the alarm's din.

My ears rang. I guess they'd been ringing all this time. I was relieved until the speakers in the ceiling clicked on. "You killed Christine! Do you believe in karma? Because that is what bad karma looks like."

The voice was male. His tone told me he was on the edge of hysteria. I pictured a smallish man with round glasses and frizzy hair. People's appearances rarely match their voices but it seemed a good bet that whoever spoke into the mic on the public address system could be a mad scientist sent over from Central Casting, complete with pocket protector.

Barnes twirled one hand above his head and our training kicked in again. We went back to back, weapons ready. Ahead of me was the elevator to Level 4. There was that sign I'd heard about: *All ye who enter here, abandon all hope.*

To my left stood large double doors that led to the lab. It was not a large space. We were stepping in Dr. Newberry's blood. I glanced at Barnes for a cue since he knew the layout of the place. He pointed right, toward the control room.

"This lab ... our company ... ," the disembodied voice said, "is called Echidna Biosystems. Echidna is from Greek myth. We chose it because Echidna was the mother of monsters. So it goes."

To my left, I heard a lock click and buzz from the entrance to the Level 3 lab. Monsters burst through the double doors and attacked.

The man on the PA system shouted, "Round one!"

EPISODE 3

Last night
I dreamt a gigantic wave
of perfect Picasso blue
crippled, crushed and swallowed
a sea of ships.
I felt the seduction of destruction
I knew the meaning of
terrible beauty.
I understood that any night
could be
the
last night.

(Artifact from the subconscious)

Two men in white lab coats sprinted out first. I raised my weapon but I hesitated. I didn't open fire but it wasn't out of mercy. I held back because I thought something might be behind them — something terrible — chasing them out, coming for us.

Lundsden fired first on the cannibal bearing down on me. Two rounds caught the infected man in the shoulder, and as a crimson flower burst across the chest of his white coat, he spun to the floor howling like a wild animal.

The other attacker, a large bellied man with a unibrow, barreled into us as I got one shot off. It was Christine Newberry's blood that really brought us down. The floor was slick with her blood. Lundsden began to fall into Davis and I reached out to catch the bomb tech. He took me and Davis with him.

Davis, like Lundsden, had been knocked flat on his back. He began to get up but the man with one eyebrow shoved him back to the floor. He clawed his way atop Lundsden, pulling at his faceplate, trying to get his hood off.

I yelled for Lundsden to watch out as I slipped to my side to grab hold of the man's collar. I worried that if I used my gun I'd shoot Davis, too. The attacker's jaws snapped at me and he bent back to close his teeth on my forearm. His eyes blazed like a rabid wolf as he bore down. He shook his head back and forth trying to get to the meat of my arm.

Still on their feet, Taylor and Barnes moved in. Taylor grabbed the man's hair and jerked his head back sharply. The Staff Sergeant did not hesitate to bring the butt of his weapon into our attacker's Adam's apple. The man's eyes rolled up and a wheezing sound creaked through his broken windpipe. Taylor still held the man's head back so Frank rammed the MP5's butt into his throat again.

Feeling clumsy in the environmental suit, I struggled to get up on my side. I didn't know if our attacker's teeth had breached my suit so I was careful to keep my forearm out of the pool of blood. Even as I got my feet under me I spotted Christine's wide eyes through her faceplate. I'd seen death before. I'd always thought the stares of the dead appeared empty but Dr. Newberry's glare was accusing.

"Is your suit torn, Harmon?" Barnes asked.

I looked up into the mouth of the Staff Sergeant's weapon.

The man with the broken throat was still struggling to breathe, clutching at his throat when Taylor tossed him aside. The dying man's heels drummed on the floor as he struggled to get air that would never come.

Taylor bent to check my suit's integrity, rotating my wrist sharply and painfully. "He's good."

"I-I'm not," Lundsden said. I could barely hear his weak voice muffled by his respirator. "My back."

When the bomb tech fell, something in his spine had gone wrong. Either his oxygen tank or the battering ram he'd slung over his shoulder had delivered a crushing blow.

"Can you move?" Barnes asked.

"Feels like my backbone is on fire but I can feel my feet. I think I can get up, but maybe I shouldn't?"

"*Can you move?*"

"Yeah … it's not that bad."

Lundsden would have been correct if that hadn't been the moment when the second wave of attackers hit us.

The mad scientist on the public address system shouted gleefully, "Round two!"

15

Two women came at us through the same double doors. Blood dripped from their gaping mouths as they howled and snarled. The way they came at us so fast — teeth bared and jaws snapping — I thought of wolves again.

I was still rising to my feet but I threw myself toward Lundsden. He screamed in pain. I managed to get us both out of their way. Barnes and Taylor didn't hesitate to open fire. They took the women down with headshots.

From a crouch, Davis rolled to his right to stay out the line of fire. If he'd rolled toward us, he would have been okay. Instead, he ended up beside the infected man Lundsden had shot. The shoulder wound wasn't enough to keep him down for good. Maybe the attacker had been playing possum. I should have put a round in his head to be sure. Had I taken that precaution, I would have saved Davis from getting his hood yanked down, then off, by the crazed screamer.

Davis's hair was plastered to his head with sweat. The straps that held his respirator in place slipped and the air mask went down to his neck. Exposed to the lab's potentially toxic environment, he panicked, scrabbling to pull the mask back up to his mouth. Though the attacker's left arm hung loose from his shoulder wound, the infected man seemed unnaturally strong and determined.

Davis finally pried his respirator from the wounded attacker's grip. He was still trying to wrestle his mask and hood back on when the Staff Sergeant shot the attacker twice in the face. The infected lab tech's head rocked back and forth as if his neck had turned to a loose spring. The man was dead before he slumped back to the floor.

Lundsden cried out from the pain.

"I'm so sorry, Bob," I said. "I had to get you out of the line of fire and away from those women."

Bob Lundsden could be an aloof know-it-all pain in the ass. Worse, sometimes he really did seem to know it all. None of that mattered. He wasn't our bomb tech anymore. He was Bob, a human being in pain. Trying to save him, I'd caused more pain. Story of my life … and death.

On the job, Steve Taylor could sometimes be a poser who thought he was G.I. Joe. Off the job, no one was more generous or funny. Hanging out with Steve, I figured out that he amped up the macho bullshit because he was the least sure of himself. He wanted to do well and to never get anything wrong. Better than doing well, he wanted to do right. When I caught his eye, even through his face-plate, his fear was obvious. We'd dealt with a lot of shit but I'd never seen him that scared.

Patrick Davis was the asshole of our squad who came off badge heavy even when he wasn't wearing the badge. He acted like he was better than the rest of us and destined to run all of the ETF one day. Moments ago, he'd pointed his weapon at me. Despite the fact that I liked Patrick least, a wave of relief washed over me when he got his respirator back on. There were still plenty of us to fight our way out of here. With Bob in agony, we were already down one man and we still had a mission.

Chest heaving, Patrick sat on his butt and took another few breaths from his respirator. He looked from the dead lab tech to Staff Sergeant Barnes and gave him a grateful nod for taking the shot. "Thanks. I'll never forget that."

Barnes shot Patrick Davis in the forehead. His head jerked back and the smacking sound of the hit startled us. Our first team member was sacrificed.

"You're welcome, Pat. I'll never forget this, either."

A bullet is a mercy compared to shitting yourself to death. Pat had said that. I guess it's better than becoming one of those screaming, mindless, infected things.

16

As I pulled Bob to his feet as gently as I could, Staff Sergeant Barnes turned his weapon on the next two attackers. These wolves were a young man and a woman of about forty. They came at us in tandem. The young man was broad and barrel-chested and came at us like a bowling ball. The woman's wet hair hung in her face so I couldn't see her eyes. She ran with the grace and speed of a gazelle.

Still recovering from shooting one of his team in the face, Barnes wasn't quite quick enough to line up the shot. Despite the close range, he missed the male attacker as he flashed by. Two of Frank's rounds chunked into the door behind my head. The projectiles spat a metallic, unyielding *bamp! Bamp!*

"Round three!" the crazed voice, so shrill and excited, knifed at us from the ceiling speakers.

Taylor didn't wait to shoulder his weapon. He fired from the hip and ripped through the male attacker's thick torso. The zombie's inertia kept him flailing forward. He clawed at Taylor as he went down and managed to grab Taylor's belt. The infected man pulled him down as Taylor punched and kicked, trying to pull away.

The attacker was in such a determined, orgiastic fugue that I spotted the whites around each bulging eye. Single-minded and seemingly starving for meat and blood, the zombie's mouth dripped with a mixture of blood and thick saliva.

The zombies seemed to know where we were most vulnerable. The infected man clutched at Taylor's faceplate and tried to pull off his hood.

Barnes turned to fire on Taylor's attacker but there was no safe shot. The Staff Sergeant spun to take the woman down by clotheslining her with his gun butt. She surprised him by nimbly ducking his outstretched arm and joining the fray against Taylor. Maybe she went for Taylor because his struggle with the other zombie had gone to the floor. Perhaps, with the pack intelligence of wolves, she zeroed in on the prey that appeared most vulnerable in that moment.

In the fight for survival, Taylor was no longer the tough G.I. Joe-type I'd known. He was Steve, yelling for help in a high trembling voice. The floor and my boots were still slick with blood. I tried to stand Bob up but he screamed from the pain and stayed bent at the waist. With Lundsden leaning on me heavily, I had to plant my feet wide so I wouldn't go down again. I was only a few feet away but I was useless to my fishing buddy.

I left it to Staff Sergeant Barnes to do the killing. He seemed to have a taste for it I lacked.

I turned my attention to Bob and pulled on the strap to get the breaching tool off his back. I let it clang to the floor. I hoped that, with the forty-pound weight of the battering ram off him, the bomb tech might prove more useful. Instead, Bob's face twisted into a mask of misery. He dropped his MP-5 and wept.

I knew what Bob wanted most in the world. It's what I wanted, too. His eyes implored me to get him out of the Box. I punched the button to open the lock so we could get out of Level 3.

It buzzed briefly but of course the hatch didn't open. I reached out with one shaky hand to turn the handle. It wouldn't budge. I glanced at the keypad outlined in glowing red numerals. In my rush, I'd forgotten I needed the manual override code to retreat and evac-

uate the wounded. I tried to remember the code. It had started with
5 - 5 - A - Z - 2 … beyond that I was in a fog.

"I'm sorry, Bob. I can't get you out until we clear this place."

"It's okay, Danny. We aren't getting out of here anyway. You
know that, right?"

1 7

The zombie under Taylor was wounded, losing the fight and beginning to lose consciousness. Steve would have been okay if not for the infected woman. She was older than Steve by at least fifteen years and he probably had seventy more pounds of muscle. As the male zombie's hands slipped from Steve's faceplate, the woman came at him at a dead run.

Coming out of a crouch in the small space, there was no time to aim and fire. Steve braced for impact, ready to be the wall so his new attacker would get knocked to the floor. Facing a much smaller opponent, I would have done the same thing. It would have worked, too, but she didn't run to collide with him. Instead, with unnatural grace and speed, the attacker yanked off his hood as she dove over him.

Steve looked to Barnes and read his expression in an instant.

"Wait! Stop!" Bob managed to yell through his pain. "He's still got his respirator on!"

True, Steve was still breathing his own air. However, his eyes and ears were exposed.

The Staff Sergeant hesitated. He shouldn't have. The woman, now behind him, reached around his head to plunge her fingers into

Steve's eye sockets as she lunged for the exposed flesh of his cheek. The zombie's eyes rolled back in ecstasy as she sank her teeth into him.

Steve let out a long keening wail that was not silenced when Barnes shot the woman in the head. With her mouth full of meat, she slumped on his shoulder and bled gore down his neck. Blinded, in pain and still thinking he was under attack, Steve yanked his pistol from his holster and the muzzle found the dead woman's skull. He pulled the trigger three times before collapsing forward, throwing her body forward atop the corpse of the bare chested attacker.

Steve was still screaming as he fired his Glock 17 three more times into the body. Two of those shots made the corpse shudder with the impact.

The last shot clipped Staff Sergeant Barnes through the shin, shattering bone and spouting a fountain of blood. He went down hard, slamming into the floor. He could have survived the wound but his suit was perforated. By his own rules, Frank Barnes had to die.

The Staff Sergeant wasn't my funny, gruff and tough superior officer anymore. Shot and in pain, he was simply Frank, now.

Steve's Glock clattered to the floor and he curled up, the heels of his hands pressed to his ruined eyes. "What's happening?"

"Your attacker is down," I said. "You did it, Steve."

Gingerly, I leaned Lundsden against the hatch to the chamber that led back to Level 2 and safety. My instinct was to get a tourniquet on Frank's wound, stanch the bleeding and somehow get the wounded out of this pit. Frank waved me away.

Bob and I looked at each other. I could tell Bob was about to tell Steve that he'd shot Frank. I shook my head hard. Bob had the good sense to shut up. My throat had gone dry. I croaked, "The Staff Sergeant is wounded, too, Steve."

"Wounded? I'm blind!" Steve groaned at what must have been monstrous pain. I would have moved to comfort him but I was the only one left who was mobile. I had to stand my ground and guard Bob. I raised my MP5 and trained it on the open doors to the lab.

Frank pulled off his hood and respirator, sucking air in and out fast. Tears cascaded down his cheeks but I don't think it was all physical pain that made him weep. "I'm sorry. I'm sorry, I'm sorry — "

"You've got nothing to be sorry about, sir," I said.

"Yeah, I do." Frank winced. "Damn, that hurts!"

I glanced down at the gaping wound.

"It burns! I didn't think a gunshot wound would burn so much, like acid and fire." He gasped for breath. "I don't think I'll feel it for much longer anyhow. Sorry I brought you guys down here."

"We go where the trouble is."

"But we aren't all here. Mac and me … we had the training to take care of this. He should be down here. The veteran officers should be down here. Mac and I thought it would be easier … better … to take the youngest on the team."

"Why?" Bob asked.

"Because I've known the rest longer. They're seasoned. I came up with the others. I golf with them. I know their wives and kids."

"You took the guys without families of their own," I said. "It's understandable."

Frank managed a grim laugh. "I took the guys on the squad I like the least."

I stared in his eyes. Those few seconds seemed to drag out a long time. When I looked away, I looked to his gushing wound again. It wasn't gushing so much anymore. He was bleeding out. Frank would die but he'd have more time to think about his sins and I was glad of it.

"I should have asked for volunteers."

"Yeah, you should have," I said.

"And briefed us better," Bob added.

"Mac thought — with what we had to do — the less you knew going in, the better."

"When is that ever true?" There was more anger than pain in Bob's voice now.

"I led the mission. It's me who messed up, *all* on me. Protecting everyone on the other side of that hatch is up to you now,

Harmon." With trembling hands he fumbled for the lanyard with the yellow laminated card. "The override code is the only way out of here. Secure this location, Danny. Kill whoever's left and get the hell out. It stinks in here."

"Frank?" Steve asked.

"Yeah?"

"You brought us down here." Taylor reached for his pistol, groping blindly. He found his weapon, raised it and pointed it in our direction.

I recoiled and fell on my back, trying to avoid blind fire. No pun intended.

Crack!

As I scrambled back to my feet I saw what he'd done. Steve shot himself in the head.

You brought us down here. His last words were not eloquent. Everyone should plan their dying words. To be safe, the message has to be short and preferably wise or kind, maybe imparting wisdom, maybe a comforting lie for the living. I say it should be that way but that's another of those lies we tell ourselves. On the day you die, you're the same dumbass who got up that morning with a head full of hopes and dreams for the future. Dying doesn't make us special.

Killing? Dying? Those are the easiest things to do in the world. Looking around me, I didn't think anybody had much of a handle on how to live, either.

18

"How is your man, the one who shot Christine?" The man on the speakers asked. "He doesn't look good."

I glanced down at Frank. His face was very pale and his breaths came fast, like that of a man running uphill, running out of wind. His eyes were rolled back in his head. While I was distracted by all the rampant death and destruction, he must have passed out.

"I'd offer to help," the voice said, "but I'm not really that kind of doctor."

"What kind are you?" I yelled.

"A bioengineer. I work on nefarious projects for multinational corporations that manufacture bio-weapons."

"I thought doctors are supposed to help people."

"Yes, well, people aren't supposed to kill people. What they tell you and how it really is are obviously two different things. The rules are loosey-goosey. Your murders are sanctioned by the state so no big deal, I guess. All things considered, it's hard to feel sorry for you. Came to kill, got killed. I'm sure my pets come as a surprise but they have the potential to be superior killers."

"Your *pets*?"

"I'm speaking fancifully but they are a lot like you on the micro scale. You're packed full of microorganisms, you know. You've got more bugs in your guts than you have cells you think of as *you*."

I looked at Bob. "This is insane."

"You know what else? You have a lot in common with my creations."

"How's that?"

"Like you, they're only doing what they were designed to do."

Bob struggled to straighten up and gasped in pain. "Are you talking about these people or the bacteria or ... what is this? Something like rabies? Is this a chemically induced psychosis?"

"Idiots talk about flying off on suicide missions to Mars but bioengineering right here is the real frontier. The parasites are alive and all they want to do is feed, reproduce and survive, like us. My work is with waterborne parasites. They take over brains. That's what Nature made them do even before I came along with some helpful tweaks."

Bob was sweating. I wasn't sure how much longer he could stand. I didn't want to have to carry him out. I tried to hurry things along. My plan was to scrub the mission and get Bob and me out after I'd gathered what information I could (as long as I could do it safely and quickly). "Brain parasites? You made brain parasites do this?"

"It would be poetic if the process wasn't so gross, don't you think?" the man replied.

"Were these people your co-workers?" I asked.

"A short time ago, yes. I'm supposed to feel bad, aren't I? The trouble is, *somebody* was going to get turned into bio-weapons. Isn't it fair that the people working so hard to develop more ways to kill people get slain by what they strove to create? Surely you don't agree that the targets should only be people who live far away? It's not nameless brown people on the news getting the shaft this time. I'm morally flexible but at least I'm not a racist, hm?"

"You're a killer," I said.

"As are you."

I hadn't killed anyone yet. I sure wanted to.

"How'd you do it?" Bob called out and it hurt him. His breath came in a wheeze. I wondered if he had a broken rib that was now poking into his lungs.

"The short answer is that I took what was and extrapolated. You wouldn't understand the long answer."

"How did you infect these people?" Bob persisted. "How did you manage any of this?"

"Are you familiar with the tongue-eating louse? It's a parasitic crustacean that infests a fish's mouth, devours the tongue and then replaces the tongue. Amazing parasite, wouldn't you say?"

"I don't see — "

"How about Scopalamine? It's also known as Devil's Breath, most popular among criminals in Columbia. It's terrifying what that drug can do. You get that powder blown in your face, and not only are you highly suggestible, you lose all memory of someone subverting your will. One dose of Devil's Breath, I could get you to help me rob your house, empty your bank accounts or shoot all your friends in the face."

"Bullshit," I said.

"Under the influence of drugs, I'm sure you're seen people do crazy things. Hurt those they love? Jump off a building?"

I had seen those things but I didn't want to admit it.

"Under stress, too, people are often surprised by what they can do. I understand. I've been under a lot of stress lately and I've surprised myself. Look around you. That's the work of weaponized parasites. They said it wasn't possible to do it to humans. My so-called superiors thought our brain chemistry was too complex to highjack."

"You must be so proud."

"They had no vision but, no matter. Nature provided my vision. *Toxoplasma gondii* is a parasite that sexually reproduces in the guts of cats. But how does it get into cat guts? The parasite alters rat brains so they aren't repelled by the scent of their predators. The rats don't run from the smell of cat urine so they get eaten. *Et voila!* More *Toxo-plasma gondii* in the world. While everyone else toyed with bacteria and viruses, I spent my days weaponizing a parasite, one that turns ordinary people into the glorious demonstration you see today: Ordinary, law-abiding people attacking police. I'm good at what I do. Very good, *singularly* good."

"This is a monster factory."

"Through the magic of biological manipulation, we are defense contractors in the business of turning enemy civilian populations into soldiers."

"Killers with no souls."

"How do you feel about 'agents of chaos?'"

"Zombies, more like it."

"Not to be pedantic, but they didn't rise from the grave or anything. Though I did enjoy those old Romero movies, I made cannibals who act remarkably like zombies. That's the brain parasite seeking to feed and reproduce. Nature's a cold-hearted bitch, hm?"

"Who are you?" I asked.

"I'm an employee … or at least, I was. Human Resources probably won't want me back for my exit interview after all this. It's okay. I don't need their references."

"What happened with the bodies on Levels 1 and 2?" Bob asked.

"Got in the way, that's all. I actually liked Tarique. That was the guard's name. Brought him coffee sometimes. I gave him a bottle of sangria last Christmas. Too bad, really, but I had to access the tanks and put some sensors into maintenance mode."

"Tanks?"

"I've got a little lab set up in my apartment. Bringing in my waterborne strain to Level 2 was easy. I dosed the water tanks. The staff showered before entering the decontamination locks. Before they ever got near the clean rooms — "

Bob let out a shallow laugh. "I get it. As the staff showered on Level 2, they thought they were going through the usual decontaminating process." Bob gripped the hatch door. He looked like he was about to slide to the floor. "They were infected before they even climbed into their biohazard suits."

"Bright boy!" The man sounded jubilant. "But I prefer the term *infested*. You can be infected by a virus. We've got those down in Level 4, too, but these pets are parasites. They're like cockroaches infesting a house, hiding in the rugs and under the fridge. Stem cells cannot cross the blood brain barrier but my pets breach the barrier, carry the nanites across and take up residence in your brain folds and crevices."

Infested is such an ugly word, I thought, *even worse than infected. That word won't stick.*

I checked my oxygen meter. We hadn't been down here thirty minutes and everything had turned to shit. I didn't want to waste any more time. "What's your name?"

"His name is Hamish," Bob said. "I forget his last name but there aren't that many guys named Hamish."

"You are correct. Hamish Allen. My name is Hamish Allen."

Bob had surprised me. I asked, "How'd you know?"

"Dr. Newberry mentioned his name, said he was senior staff on site. Listen to how this guy talks. He's gotta be the guy running things. You can't talk like that and be a grunt."

"You are bright," Hamish said. "I'm the one in charge when people with more money aren't around. Are you a hazardous materials expert, sir?"

"I'm a bomb disposal specialist," Bob said.

"Ah. In a way, I guess we're both bomb disposal specialists."

A small security camera was fixed on me. I looked straight into the lens as if I could see the man in the control room. "Are you willing to come out, Hamish?"

"Sure. You're what I've been waiting for. I couldn't disable all the sensors. I need your override code to get out."

"Come out then."

"Shoot the man on the floor first."

Frank Barnes snorted and one weepy eye fluttered open. He had been listening, after all. "No."

"You want me to shoot Staff Sergeant Barnes?" I asked. "He's already down! He's no threat to you. Why on — "

"Not like this!" Frank said. His anger burbled up first, then he began to weep.

"I need to know you understand who's in control here," Hamish said. "You've got the guns. I've got something better. I've got a pocketful of miracles and a skull packed with secrets. Shoot him or I'll unleash another bioengineered miracle. You and the bomb disposal specialist can eat each other."

"You'd be stuck down here."

"They'll send someone else along in a short while. Next time I'll try playing victim. I'll tell them I have the cure. They'll escort me out and give me a blanket. The people who own this place don't want the research to be destroyed and I've got it all in my head."

"Don't do this," Frank pleaded.

He was crying. I was, too, a little.

"He's as good as dead anyway, Dan," Bob said.

"You said it was in the shower water!" I argued. "It's in the water! We didn't go through the showers on Level 2!"

"I'm sorry. I had orders!" Frank said. "I killed the wrong people for the wrong reasons. I'm sorry!"

Before I could reply, a shot rang out.

I whirled to discover that Frank hadn't been talking to me.

Bob leaned against the wall, his pistol drawn. He'd shot Frank in the head.

"Like the man said, I'm pretty bright. I did the math in my head. At least the Staff Sergeant got a chance to apologize for being a shithead."

20

I looked down at Frank. Despite all the blood loss, it looked like he still had plenty of fluid flowing from his skull. The pool of blood expanded to join the rest of the flood smeared across the floor. They say the body is up to 60% water. Sometimes on the job we used the term *meat bags* for the dead. We are bags of blood.

"Forgive the bright boy," Hamish said over the intercom. "He knows what's up."

I looked down at the yellow card in my hand. The lanyard, once blue, was wet and dark with spray. "How should I handle this, Bob?"

"Give him the override code, Danny. I'm tired."

I couldn't think of any way to stall until a better idea came along. Our oxygen was more than half gone. Bob didn't look good. It would be bug out time soon, no matter what. I might salvage the mission if I could take Hamish out as a prisoner. "I'll tell you the code, Hamish. Key it in on the keypad on your side and open that door. Understand?"

"What's not to understand?"

I gave Bob a long look. "I'm going to get us out of here."

He could barely lift his head to look my way. "Doubtful."

I put some bass in my voice to address the doctor. "When the door buzzes, come out slowly, hands up where we can see them."

Hamish laughed. "You still think you're driving this bus?"

"Come out so we can talk and get it over with." Bob sounded exhausted. Or maybe that was the tone of a man resigned to death.

"Good lads," he said. "I'm all for getting out of here as quickly as possible. Look around you. This place isn't good for your health!"

I'd seen enough horrors today to last for this lifetime and into the next. It was the "good lads," thing that made me want to become a wolf. Hamish's arrogance made me want to become one of his weapons so I could turn on him without hesitation, without thought or consequence. I wanted to tear off his ears with my teeth as I closed my hands around his throat. I wanted to choke that smug laugh out of him. Becoming a remorseless murderer would make everything so simple … or so I thought at the time.

I'd taken an introductory course to negotiation tactics. I knew I was supposed to keep him calm. I wasn't supposed to allow the situation to escalate his fear. The trouble was, Hamish Allen didn't sound scared in the least. "Give me the code twice. Speak loud, slowly and clearly. Doctor's orders!"

You can't bluff when you don't have any cards. I did as I was told. "5 - 5 - A - Z - 2 - 5 - 0 - 0 - L - 1 - 1 - V - 3 - T - P - D - Q 5 - 5 - A - Z - 2 - 5 - 0 - 0 - L - 1 - 1 - V - 3 - T - P - D - Q."

Hamish repeated the code back to me twice. It didn't occur to me he was stalling.

Like everybody, I've made a lot of mistakes in my life. Some highlights: I chose a university based on the fact that it had the shortest application form. I wrapped my first car around a tree when I took a corner too fast, showing off for buddies in the back seat. I first got into law enforcement because a girl who cheated on me said I'd look sexy in the uniform. I told myself I liked my job. I told myself that even if I hated it, I was committed to the Toronto Police Service for life.

Doing as Dr. Hamish Allen told me was another big mistake.

Ding!

"Here I come!" Hamish shouted.

I could have used the override code to open the control room door myself. Instead, Hamish used the code — the code *I* gave him — to raise the elevator from level 4. I didn't even know what he was really up to, yet. I didn't have time to think about that as Hell boiled up from the bottom of the Box.

EPISODE 4

Two men burst from the elevator followed by a large woman. Their protective hoods were off. They'd splattered green puke down the front of their white environmental suits.

Hamish, still safely behind the control room door, cackled over the PA system. "Gentlemen, meet Natalie, Glen and Arthur! *Dinnertime!*"

I stood closest to the elevator doors as they parted. The area was not a large space and the attackers came at us fast. I should have been the next to die. The infested would have attacked me if it hadn't been for Bob.

The biggest man slammed me and I went down hard. My head bounced off the floor. As my MP5 clattered to the floor and spun away, a high whine shot through my ears. Everything seemed to slow down for a moment. Like wolves, all three pounced on the easiest prey first. As they rushed to get at Bob, he slid to the floor while firing his pistol. He might have hit one of them but they soon knocked the Glock from his hand. They were too fast. Bob was too injured to defend himself.

The woman leaped atop him first, pawing at his faceplate. Her angry growling sounded borne of starvation. One of the men pinned his arms as my teammate let out a scream. His body contorted under their attack. I guessed that whatever had cracked and shifted in his spine was now grinding nerve-rich fractured bone ends together. Pain ripped through him.

One of the men got his hood off. Then the drooling killer began to rip into Bob's throat. Bob screamed until his windpipe opened.

I was trying to get to my feet when the man holding Bob's legs wheeled and jumped on top of me. He was heavy but I had one knee under me. I managed to flip him to the floor. He kept rolling. I found myself on the floor face up. I managed to wrap my right arm around the back of my attacker's neck and curl around to trap his head in my right armpit.

Biohazard suits are not ideal for hand-to-hand combat. It was slippery, awkward work. I didn't have much time to end the fight before the others would turn their murderous attention to me. I didn't want to be the object of their blood frenzy. If it came to that, I'd shoot myself first.

My sidearm was on my right hip. I tried to make a quick grab for it with my left hand. I could barely get hold of the pistol grip before my attacker grabbed my wrist.

Struggling to keep him at bay, I could see Frank's Glock out of the corner of my eye to my right, just out of reach. I tried to haul my assailant toward it but I didn't have enough leverage to budge him sideways.

I tried kicking my legs out, rocking us both upwards. I held no hope that I could stand us both up. However, I did manage to slam his face into the floor as we fell back down. The man grunted in pain. At least these monsters felt something. I had to inflict more pain, *all* the pain. I tried the same maneuver, kicking my legs up again. When he resisted, I allowed his momentum and weight to carry us back down to the tile floor. His face made a wet smack on impact.

On my next attempt, the man finally got wise and tried to twist sideways. We rolled a little closer toward Frank's Glock. If I broke my grip to reach for my own pistol, the cannibal would yank my hood off and make me more vulnerable to his teeth. I would have to take him out with my bare hands and quickly.

Then I remembered a lecture from a visiting trainer on loan from the RCMP. Exoculation is not standard procedure but one of the trainers had stuck his fingers in an attacker's eyes. "Don't hesitate and go for it if you need to," the constable had said. "If you commit, you'll go in to the second knuckle."

I let my attacker out of the headlock. As he rose up, I pushed into his eyes with my thumbs. I didn't perform the attack exactly as it had been described to me but it did the grisly job. My attacker reeled back, clutching his eyes. The man curled up. In his agony, he arched his back at an alarming angle I didn't know was possible for an overweight office worker. He let out a high screech, went rigid and collapsed to the floor, apparently unconscious.

If I were a different person, maybe I would have felt a few seconds of triumph over an enemy bent on killing me. A feeling of relief would not have been out of order. Instead, a wave of revulsion pulsed through my guts. I almost threw up into my respirator.

That's what that woman did to Steve! I'm becoming one of them!

But I wasn't infested yet. I was a man fighting off bloodthirsty monsters. I was struggling to remain a human.

They warned us about letting emotions rule us in training. "When you roll up on a scene, maintain officer neutrality. Do the same when you go home. Leave the troubles of the job at the job."

We saw people do terrible things to each other every day. A lot of cops get angry about that and they stay angry. Sometimes we take that anger out on spouses or even our kids. Maybe we start drinking and fail to figure out how to stop.

"We send you out on the streets with a whip and a chair to be lion tamers. Don't join the lions."

Another trainer added, "And if you figure out how to deal with the stress, let me know how you did it because I'm not sure, either. At some point you're going to see something that messes with your head. Your head might stay messed up. On your best days, you'll feel like you're saving the world. On your worst days, you'll feel like the world isn't worth the effort."

It was my attacker's pained screaming that got the zombies off Bob. Their heads rose from his still body. They turned to look at me. Jaws covered in blood, the man and the woman broke into broad red smiles.

I almost pissed myself. My head still buzzed and ached from my concussion. Forgetting the pistol in my holster, I panicked. I needed to create space between me and the threat. I wanted my submachine gun in my hands.

The man and woman sprang to their feet as I backpedaled toward my MP5. I would have been fine except for all the blood on the floor. Bob, Frank, Patrick, Steve and Christine Newberry fed the pool. Fresh blood on a tile floor is as slippery as soap. Crabbing backward on my heels and palms, I slipped and slid.

After the pain of being torn apart and eaten alive, what awaited me? Darkness? Nothingness? A heavenly choir and a harp? David Bowie jamming with Elvis and John Lennon? I hoped Lemmy from Motorhead would be there, too. He was more to my musical taste.

Questions about the afterlife used to be so theoretical. The answer was coming fast.

The zombies didn't step over the dead. They stepped on the bodies of Christine Newberry and Frank Barnes as they came for me.

2 2

Until that moment, I'd only had the bad kind of luck. However, as they stepped down from Frank's face and chest, the slick floor slowed the monsters, too. They didn't seem to mind falling much. Both of them crawled across the floor. Coming at me like that, it was impossible not to think of them as wild animals. My MP5 lay against the wall. I might get to it in time, but I might not. My hand closed on my pistol.

Everyone on the team used Glocks with rubberized pistol grips. It was supposed to be a measure against sweat. Today, it helped me avoid dropping my weapon back into the blood. The female attacker was faster than the male. At the last moment, she surprised me by leaping, apparently intent on landing atop me as she had with Bob. I raised my weapon and fired. I had no time to aim but a pink mist blossomed like a halo from the back of her exploding skull. She was dead before her body fell on my legs.

My brain already felt like a pea rattling around in a matchbox. The report of the gunshot in such a tight space made my ears whine louder.

The last attacker was a man who did not seem the least deterred by the fact that I'd taken out two of his pack. He crawled over her to get at me. He seemed to know the gun in my hand was a weapon. These zombies were not the shuffle and moan variety. There was intelligence behind his eyes. He grabbed my wrist and bashed my hand against the floor. I tried to drive a knee into his ribs but the weight of the dead woman was on my legs.

He bashed my hand against the floor and I triggered it by accident. This time the gun went off beside my right ear. A few inches the wrong way and I would have shot myself in the head. The walls seemed to vibrate with the roar of the report. My headache had been a painful throb that matched the pace of my racing heart. Now it felt like I was trying to hear my thoughts above the roar of a jet engine.

I tossed the gun so I'd have a free hand to grapple. My attacker lunged with his teeth. I punched a couple of knuckles into his sternum to make some room to move. The sternum is nerve-rich and sensitive but half-measures weren't doing the trick. He raised both fists and began beating my faceplate with whaling fists like a gorilla in one of those *Planet of the Apes* movies.

I could only try to block the man's blows. The long, slim oxygen tank on my back was digging into the space between my shoulder blades. I gritted my teeth against the pain. I was weakening. I couldn't keep him off me forever. The adrenaline raging through my bloodstream slowed my perception even further. Soon, I was sure, he'd pull my hood off. The blows rained down on my forearms like the zombie was pounding timpani.

I looked at the man's bloody maw. He'd chewed on Bob. Those same teeth could open my flesh at any moment. I gave up hope in that moment. It was almost as if I was watching my unfolding murder happen to someone else. When one relents, when a victim's death as inevitable, it is a dreamlike state.

Then a stranger thing happened. The zombie was forming words. No sound passed his lips but he was mouthing something. Even as he continued to try to kill me, he mouthed a message. I was almost sure he was trying to say, "I'm sorry, I'm sorry. I'm sorry." Not that it mattered. Each apology was accompanied by a fresh wild swing, punctuating each impact.

Exhausted and ready to die, I didn't hear the door buzz open. I didn't see who picked up Frank's Glock. I only felt the reverberation of the gunshots pound into my head as my attacker took three to the chest. The man fell back dead, adding weight to my legs, pinning me under two bodies.

Maybe I'll live.

My little flame of hope was quickly extinguished as I saw a man in a blood-spattered white coat gather weapons from the fallen and toss them though the open door to the control room. When that was done, he slammed it closed and the lock buzzed again.

"Dr. Allen, I presume?"

He pointed Frank's pistol my way. "Got that right, buddy."

I tried to get up on one elbow to get a better look at him. Hamish was medium: medium height, build and looks. I expected a sweaty maniac in a biohazard suit. Instead, he was calm and methodical, just another man, utterly unremarkable except for his ugly paisley shirt.

Hamish retrieved the yellow card from the bloody floor, stepped over me to punch the elevator button. "Stay down. I'll be right back. If you're good, I'll give you some answers to your questions. This whole thing … I know how it looks but this isn't even what you think it is. Believe it or not, I'm the good guy."

He checked the time on his phone. "We have a little time left — not much — but it's almost over."

Ding!

23

I struggled to get out from under the two bodies weighing down my legs. My head pounded. It was as if the blood in my head was squeezing past the bite of a vise at my temples. I rocked back and forth to get out from under the dead. That done, I slipped over to my side and grunted like an old man trying to get to my feet.

I have since learned that people infested with weaponized brain parasites are very sensitive to sound. Like a flock of bats, they will turn as one when they detect noise. Hearing is more important than sight. I had confirmation of this as I got to my feet. The attacker whose eyes I'd taken came at me in a rush on all fours, jaws snapping.

The zombie's ruined eyes seemed to stare at me. For a second, I was transfixed. I only had that second before his teeth closed on my calf. I stepped aside quickly and kicked him in the ribs. He grunted but seemed undeterred. I went to the edge of the room where the blood spill was most sparse. I was careful to avoid treading on Bob's body, and as I leapt over the man and woman who'd attempted to murder me, it crossed my mind that they might come back to life and join the chase.

My life is a horror movie. My death would be worthy of a horror movie.

The wolf at my heels either didn't see the corpses he climbed over or didn't mind them.

I had a moment of inspiration and stopped running. Instead, I tiptoed to the middle of the room. I took a deep breath and held it as I stepped atop Frank's body and stood still.

The zombie's jaws dripped saliva in long strings as it kept crawling in circles around the room. As suddenly as it had come at me, it stopped to sniff the air. There was such a mix of blood and gore and death, I didn't think he could track me by smell. The dead not only look drunk, as I mentioned, they're messy drunks. As soon as the sphincters loosen, they shit themselves.

I was reminded of this fact when I shifted my weight on my team leader's guts and the corpse let out a long fart. I would have laughed — grimly and bitterly — except the infested thing trying to kill me snapped his head my way. Tentatively, he crawled my way, sniffing the air.

My lungs burned for air. I glanced at the control room door to my right. What was the override code? Trying to remember the alphanumeric sequence felt like a physical strain. Of course, I was so freaked out, I'm not sure I could have come up with my sister's phone number. Jenn was an EMT in Mississauga. I would have loved to come up with the code so I could escape through the hatch and leave Hamish to deal with his creation. I could get the hell out and, in my fantasy, Jenn would be waiting for me in her ambulance. She'd drive me far away. I'd lie down in back and I'd never think of the Box again.

But what was the code? 5 - 5 - A - Z - 2 … dammit!

My lips began to tremble. Beneath my mask, my face felt hot. Warm sweat trickled down my back. I reached for my belt searching for something useful. I had ammo mags and a first aid kit but I didn't even have my telescoping baton. Maybe I could beat on the zombie with my handcuffs but what I really wanted was my knife. I normally carried a retractable blade but orders were to leave our knives in the truck. When we trained in biohazard suits, we were told to leave our edged weapons behind. Knives slice and cut.

Serrated edges tear. They didn't want us slicing our gloves or protective suits.

In hindsight, that was a decision made by a higher-up who would never be in my situation. We had guns but they wouldn't trust us with knives if we wore our blue Hazmats? Ridiculous, but mindless bureaucracy can be as dangerous as any cannibal starving for human flesh.

My lungs were on fire now. I couldn't hold my breath any longer. I let go of the old air to suck in the new. My respirator clicked. It was enough for the eyeless monster to zero in on me. I should have broken the bastard's eardrums.

The locked control room door stood to my right. Behind me was Bob's corpse and the hatch to Level 2. To my left, the double doors leading to the Level 3 labs stood open. I almost ran that way until I noticed the one weapon Hamish had failed to lock away. Bob's body lay atop the battering ram.

As the infested man crawled forward, I stepped off Frank and bent to reach for the breaching tool. One end was a blunt hammerhead. The other end came to an edge thin enough to cram into the crack of a door. It would open the blind zombie's skull quite efficiently. However, to get at it, I'd have to turn my back to the attacker and take the time to roll Bob aside.

As I bent forward, the zombie — still on all fours and coming fast as a rabid dog — rushed forward. As soon as he came to Frank's corpse, he launched himself at me. There was no time for the battering ram. I whirled and swept my forearm up like a club. I caught the killer under the jaw. He reeled back, clutching at his throat. He landed on the floor hard. I thought he'd stay down but, shakily, he got to his feet. Hurt but still hungry, he edged forward, hands extended, coming back for more.

There was little time for the battering ram. Inspiration struck. I yanked at the straps to Bob's oxygen tank and lifted it out of its pouch. It wasn't as heavy as the ram. It was harder to hold as well. With clumsy fingers, I yanked at the hose to get enough slack to use it as a bludgeon.

The attacker was almost on me. I heard a rasp in his throat. I might have lacerated something in there, pushed the hyoid bone out of whack. The hyoid anchors the muscles of the tongue and holds the larynx open. I didn't have much slack from the air hose so I struck the attacker in the same spot. A solid throat punch can ruin anybody's day. Doing it with an oxygen tank instead of a fist was a decisive move.

Gurgling, the blind monster sank to his knees. I could bash his head now and I was motivated. He went down. I kept bashing him in the head. Blood sprayed all over my suit and faceplate until it was hard to see.

My enemy was blind. I fell into a blind rage. He stayed down but I kept pummeling him with the oxygen tank until the crunching sounds became merely wet. At that, my fury left me.

The Box taught me something about myself. You can only get so full of rage. There is a limit to how much terror you can feel. After so much gore and horror, all my emotional meters had redlined and were broken. I was too exhausted to feel more anger and fear. Moments before, I'd felt resigned to death. I still didn't want to feel pain but death sounded like a relief, like escape. Now I was too tired to care. I guess the body's system can only pump out so much adrenaline. When that was burnt out, I wanted to fall into a dreamless sleep.

Getting the override code and remembering it would have solved all my problems. Since I couldn't do that, I took it out on some guy who probably stopped at Tim Horton's that morning. He probably picked up a double double and vanilla dip donut. This morning, this killer had been just another person in a city of people going about their lives.

Once he was dead, I began to see him as the victim he really was. He wasn't an it anymore. What had his name been? Hamish had said the people in the basement were … who were they again? Was one of them named Glen?

Sorry, Glen. Sorry, everybody. I wish you'd gone to Timmy's and left it at that.

Ding!

24

The elevator doors parted. "Wowie, man! Looks like you had a bonus round." In one hand, Hamish carried a hexagonal aluminum box about the size of a beer cooler. My Glock was in his other hand. The doctor peered down the barrel at me to take careful aim at my head. "Put it down."

I dropped the bloody oxygen tank to the floor with a clang. "Shit."

Hamish sized me up. "Yes, you'll do nicely."

"I'm Daniel," I said. "My friends call me Danny."

"Don't care. We aren't going to be going to ballgames, drinkin' Moosehead and grilling steak together."

"Talk to me for a minute."

"A smart man would ask if there is a way to stop the spread of the outbreak."

"Okay. Is there a vaccine?"

"A repellant, and," he tapped his temple, "only I know the formula for the water-borne vector. Other variations were the purview of ... well ... all these dead people and a few others."

"Other variations? You people were doing more with this stuff?"

"That is the best question you've asked. It gets to the crux of the matter." He nodded toward the control room. "They were pretty squirrelly about our research data. I crashed and smashed the server for good here. Fried the backups in the vault downstairs, too."

"That's what you were doing down there?"

"Among other things. Thanks for your help. Couldn't have done it without you."

"You seem to be the man with the plan."

"And all the answers." Hamish gestured to the bodies of his former co-workers. "Those were some brilliant researchers, a good team. They had all the answers, too. Unfortunately, their answers were very dangerous. Maybe someday we'll figure out how to neutralize our deadly creations but that day is far off. I'm telling you this so you understand that, for all of humanity to survive, you can't kill me. If you understand, say yes."

"Yes, you killed them all for insurance."

"My survival was one reason but I'm more altruistic than you give me credit for. My knowledge is quite singular, I assure you. I need to walk out of here safely. *You* need me to get out safely."

"You must have gotten to know the staff. How does that feel to know what you've done to them? To their families?"

"Necessary. It feels necessary. You undoubtedly think I'm some kind of cartoon villain. Not at all."

I glanced at the bodies surrounding us. "If you aren't a monster, I don't know what is."

"Then you don't know what is. You're confusing an ought with an is."

"What?"

"I'm saving the world, Daniel."

"How do you figure?"

"Do you even know what this place is?"

I shrugged. "You study diseases."

"We *weaponize* diseases," he huffed. "All these people you think of as victims made a living from turning nature's worst into man's worst. That's how all these nice people were paying for their lattes, their kids' private schools, their mortgages on nice homes in Rosedale — "

"You did this."

"I literally gave them a taste of their own medicine. These so-called victims were monsters before my pets went to work on them. Imagine a whole city's civilian population tearing each other apart, no missiles, no radiation. They would allow every man, woman and child to go at each other. Then they'd surround an enemy city and shoot whoever comes out. That was the operating theory anyway. Burn the bodies, clean up the blood and you've got a whole new city to occupy without knocking down a single building."

"You're describing a war crime."

"There's a lab like this one in nearly every major city. Everybody's trying to figure out how to make the next war crime happen. Did you really think all these labs were discovering something new and useful about bubonic plague? We study the deadly sins, not to cure them, but to use them in warfare."

"You worked here, too," I said. "What changed, Hamish? You get religion?"

"Thanks to emerging technologies, there was a breakthrough of sorts." He nodded to the box in his hand, the one that didn't hold my gun. "They borrowed some goodies from one of the company's medical subdivisions. The bioengineering is called AFTER. It has the potential to save the world but most likely, people being people, it will end everything. If it weren't for that, I would have left well enough alone. Believe me, AFTER's nanotech takes bio-weaponry beyond the next level."

"Nanotech?"

"This demonstration … heh … this *demon*-stration … " He let out that shrill laugh again. "Demons, get it? I thought you — "

"What do you mean next level?"

"With this tech, a brilliant researcher extrapolated beyond my wildest dreams and darkest nightmares. AFTER's nano engine took my elegant, targeted solutions up to something far more sinister and harder to control. I deal in microorganisms and gene splicing. Put my waterborne brain parasites together with the little robots and you've got the marriage from Hell."

"Speak plain English."

"Organo-nanites. They put another division's nanotech together with my weaponized parasites. With my work, the outbreak is confined to one water supply. Outside a host, the little buggers die. They wanted a 70% casualty rate. If our work with rhesus monkeys is a straight correlation, they've got it. I told them 70% is still too high to shoot for."

"Why that number?"

"The military objective was to sow chaos so no defense could be mounted. They weren't satisfied with making everyone drop dead. They wanted enemy populations — civilians — to turn on each other. Make the majority killers and the uninfested will become the hunted. It's too much. If you want a dragon to defend your castle, you gotta keep that thing on a leash and make sure he's tamed so he always works for you. Somebody has to shut this madness down. I'm somebody."

"A real humanitarian."

"Better than them, man. I built them a bio-bomb, sure. My pets could turn a city inside out. The bosses weren't satisfied with that. Now we're dealing with the equivalent of a nuclear explosion that could spread around the planet. With their plan, the epidemic could spread around the planet. I voiced my concerns. I warned them this was an evil genie they couldn't stuff back in the bottle. I was ignored."

"So you decided to kill everyone you worked with plus my squad?"

"My colleagues were overconfident in their ability to control their new bio-bomb. What if the organo-robotic limits fail? They were sure they'd figure it out but, in the meantime, the nanites proved less than 100% dependable."

"This is all above my pay grade — "

"Funny," Hamish said. "When I raised my objections, that's exactly what they told me. 'Above my pay grade.' This is the end of a long, dirty road that started with turning noise into a weapon. I'm sure, in your line of work, you're familiar with sound cannons."

"LRADs, yeah. What about them?"

He blew a raspberry at me, loud and long. "LRAD, as in Long-range Acoustic Device. Makes it sound like it would be good at an outdoor concert, doesn't it?"

"It's crowd control," I said. "Better than wading into a crowd with batons and shields and cracking skulls."

"Police used the LRAD on protesters at the G-20 Summit in Pittsburgh. Sonic weapons shouldn't be used on peaceful protesters, Daniel, but deafening people and the potential for permanent damage is nowhere near the point. Maybe you got what you wanted for crowd control but here's the problem: Weapons development never ends with the least effective dose."

"What else have they got brewing?"

"For one silly instance, the military research branched into trying to turn enemy forces gay and irresistibly horny."

I let out a hollow chuckle. "Not a thing."

"The experiments were unsuccessful but they really did try to make that happen. My point is, there's nothing they won't do. Go farther down that road and you find me, down here, double double, toil and trouble."

"This is your life's work, isn't it? Why turn around now?"

"I've got kids. I see where this road leads. Somebody has to say when enough is enough. My colleagues found a way to take my work to the next level. What they made is unacceptable."

"The word, 'unacceptable,' sounds weird coming from a guy willing to wipe out a city by poisoning their water supply."

"*Airborne*, Daniel! One contained vector of disease could be a precision tool that could end a war. To give brain parasites some robotic assistance and hope the weapon won't mutate further? To place all your faith in a vaccine for your population while committing genocide against all others? They're very clever but they aren't at all smart. They don't even have that vaccine yet, just the faith they can limit the effects using the nanites."

"I don't — "

"Before the first test of the nuclear bomb there was concern among some scientists that the explosion could ignite all the oxygen in the atmosphere and kill the planet instead of a couple of Japanese cities. Do you know how they ruled out that possibility with certainty?"

"I dunno. Math?"

"Wrong. They detonated Trinity and hoped for the best. That moment right there defines the best and worst of humanity. Curious, creative, inventive and too damn stupid to be half cautious."

He lifted the box and raised his voice to a shout, "That was a nuclear weapon. I hold in my hand the end of the world, a living weapon."

"What are you going to do with it, Hamish?"

"I'm going to destroy it, of course."

"The world?"

"No, you idiot! The world is where I keep all my classic vinyl of Creedence Clearwater Revival. I'm destroying the contents of this box, the wicked research and all the evil people behind it."

"So kill it and let's call it a day."

"I have to get it out of here to kill it. There can't even be any puzzle pieces left for anyone to try to put together. I love my daughters and I love, love, love my Creedence. We gotta keep the good shit goin'. I want my daughters to live on a hospitable planet. I want them to live and grow up and, when they listen to *Bad Moon Rising*, they'll remember their dad as the man who saved the world."

I looked at Frank and wished I'd had the balls to shoot him myself. I looked at Steve and Bob and wanted to cry. Patrick was kind of a prick so I didn't feel much of anything for him. Christine seemed nice. All these others? God, what a bloodbath. It did appear to me the waterborne parasites were bad enough. Their kill ratio seemed higher than seventy percent.

"Well? Do you see where I'm coming from, Daniel?"

"Well," I admitted, "I still hate your guts but I do have some mixed emotions."

"Attaboy."

2 6

Hamish told me to get into the decontamination chamber to go to Level 2. He waved my Glock at me so I did as I was told. While the air cycled and the washers and sprayers hosed us down again, we stayed on opposite ends of the chamber. Hamish didn't let down his guard but he was talkative. "Can you guess what the big three bosses of this lab are doing right now?"

"Christine said they were away."

"Ah, Christine. She trained at Johns Hopkins, came here from the CDC. She was with the Epidemic Intelligence Service. She had the brains to work on curing cancer with nanotech someday. Nice woman, to all appearances."

"But?"

"Everyone has blind spots. People get sidetracked. When Christine was in high school, she wanted to win a Nobel prize. Then she heard what work in the cleanroom of a weapons manufacturer pays."

"So you decided she needed to die so you could do this."

"You lot killed her, actually. I was watching from the control room. How do you feel about that?"

"My superiors ordered me down here because of what you did. You were talking about your bosses. Where did they go?"

"Aruba, to attend a conference of thought leaders. Sam Harris is delivering the keynote and Foo Fighters will play a private concert. They'll talk about climate change and how to turn the Sahara into farmland. The thought leaders from this lab will be discussing the dangers of nanotech and Artificial Intelligence. You know what? They'll talk so earnestly, too, like kindly and concerned grandfathers. One of our company's divisions is working on perfecting drones that could swarm a city. They could search and destroy targets based on what Facebook groups they belong to. These people are psychopaths with no sense of irony."

"Sounds like you don't like your bosses much. There's a support group for that. It includes everyone who has a boss or has ever had a boss."

"But my immediate boss, as one example, is a man named Thomas Dill. He's so rich, it's sick. He collects paintings that should be in museums so anyone can see them. Art is fine but spending millions on a painting when a copy looks the same and is so cheap has never made sense to me."

"So he likes things and you like other things. That's how things work, Hamish."

"You don't understand. Thomas sees himself as a modern day Prometheus, bringing fire to mankind. He thinks overwhelming weapons will bring all our enemies to heel. We'll never have to negotiate and can do what we want because we are as gods. You can't scare people into submission, though ... not for the long-term. Gods should rule by love, not fear. If we scare them enough, they'll just get hold of the same tech and use it against us. All Thomas remembers about Prometheus is he brought fire to humanity. He forgets fire also brought forged weapons and war. Prometheus literally means *foresight*. The people who run labs like this have no foresight."

As the sprayers hosed me down, I searched for some weakness I could exploit, some common ground that would get me out of the Box alive. "Sounds like we feel much the same about our bosses."

Hamish nodded. "We all want to control our fate. That's the

origin of most stress, feeling like you're out of control. Of course, nobody's really in control of much. That's what these people don't understand. They think they can let the genie out of the bottle and stuff it back in when they want? That's never been true. Once we went nuclear, we had to continue."

"Sounds like you regret loading their gun. The weapon you say you hate so much is based on your work."

"I do regret it. We're fighting the wrong wars. We created antibiotics and declared victory over microorganisms. Meanwhile, the microscopic war went on without us. The bacteria keep evolving and adapting so we're running out of effective antibiotics. You can't get a gallbladder removed without worrying the hospital stay will kill you."

"You're making me antsy about getting an ingrown toenail, Hamish."

"You should be nervous. Staph infections, MRSA, Clostridium difficile … we're so casual about the ordinary, everyday horrors. Necrotizing fasciitis is rare but it won't be rare forever. I've studied ebola in Liberia. I've seen bodies piled up in the center of a village, burned like cordwood. Here, you can live your entire life and manage to avoid seeing one dead body. We've forgotten what reality is. We lock the elderly and the dying out of sight and out of the way. We worship youth but people are young for a really short time. Death is Life, Daniel. We've blinded ourselves to reality."

I pointed to the shiny box. "But you think you're making the world safer by taking that out of containment?"

"I'm taking a loaded gun away from toddlers," he said. "A person in your profession should understand that."

"You say everyone has blind spots. What are yours? Did all these people really have to die?"

"No point in taking their weapon away if they can go make more. Besides, logistically, it was easy to get in here but it's much harder to subvert the sensors on the way out. To get out, I needed the master override code to turn off the system safeties. Anyone with clearance can get down here but walking out with this little box of horrors is a trial."

I could feel the heat in my cheeks and scalp, so hot with embarrassment that I wanted to yank off my gear then and there. Hamish subverted the lockdown with the master code I delivered into his hands. "You're such a smart guy, why not go away and work in a new lab somewhere else? Go cure cancer."

"Daniel, Daniel, Daniel. Don't you see? I'm curing cancer as we speak." He hefted the box. "*This* cancer."

My ears popped. The washers and sprayers finished their work and I opened the hatch to step into Level 2.

EPISODE 5

Breakdown (noun)

Crisis; collapse of a system (societal, technological and/or nervous) that can no longer sustain its illusions and/or delusions.

Lockdown (noun)

The attempt to contain a systemic failure and maintain illusions and/or delusions.

Fakedown (noun)

The purposeful assertion of delusions in order to install or maintain a failed system; arch. *propaganda.*

Wakedown (noun)

Succumbing to fakedown due to exhaustion or despair; the failure of proponents of hope to continue to act as if hope is not illusory.

~ **Notes from NEXT**

27

My head still throbbed with unrelenting pain. I'd had two concussions before. At 16, I was checked into the boards playing hockey. My second brain scramble laid me out after a bar fight in Chinatown West. I wanted to lie down now, go to sleep and wake up in my bed at home. I wanted all this to be a nightmare, easily dismissed, soon forgotten. Steve would call and we'd go fishing on the weekend. I'd study for my negotiator's course. If *normal* meant going back to blissful ignorance, I was all for going back to stupid.

"Daniel? You're swaying. Stand up and stay up. I need you conscious and functioning a bit longer. This is already hard enough."

"What's next? Somebody else will recreate the research. Your bosses knows what the research is all about. You gonna kill them, too?"

"The directors are venture capitalists and lobbyists. They only know the broad strokes. It wouldn't be bad if they died but they lack the necessary expertise to recreate organo-nanotech. They haven't stepped into the Level 4 lab since the day of its opening ceremony. The real work was done in vault labs. For all their sponsorship of the science of organo-nanotech, they're about as relevant as the CEOs of Coke or Pepsi."

Hamish directed me to the locker room. From where I stood, I could still see a trail of blood leaking across the floor from the dead man in the changeroom.

"Pay no attention to the man behind the curtain," Hamish said.

"What did he do?"

"Told you. Got in the way. That was Cal Whedon. He questioned what I was doing, fiddling with the shower tank — "

"When you dosed these showers with your parasites."

Hamish bobbed his head. "Tank maintenance was his job. When I opted not to go through the shower, Cal had to be silenced."

"There was a woman bleeding on the front step, too — "

"I saw on the security cam. You guys shot her."

"Not my decision."

"We all feel like most decisions are made for us, isn't that so? I feel that way. A conscience is a terrible nuisance, isn't it? Or do you have a conscience?"

"Who was that woman?"

"Myra Wilcox, the Level 4 lab equipment supervisor. She walked in on me knifing Cal. She came at me. I had to stab her in the side. I hesitated, you know. It was a heat of the moment thing. She was the nicest of all the staff. I suppose I should have finished what I started."

Damn. Know-it-all Bob was right about her wound.

"I let all the staff on Level 1 go. They ran out screaming after I shot the man in the closet."

"They trampled a woman on the way out."

"Yes. Karen Gardener. I don't think it was the trampling. Heart attack, probably. I would have helped her if I hadn't been in a rush. Most of them didn't know anything top secret. They thought we were looking for treatments for anthrax. That was the official line. Karen worked in procurement of lab animals. I'm pretty sure she had no idea she worked for a weapons manufacturer."

I was running out of patience. "What do you want from me, man?"

"Your nice blue environmental suit, Daniel."

"There are plenty of suits down here."

"Not like yours. I need that dark blue biohazard suit."

"You're going to dress up like me — "

"And escape in the isolation van."

"If I say no — "

"I'll shoot you in the foot and I'll have to yank it off you while you scream."

"Use one of my teammate's Hazmats for your disguise."

He let out an exasperated sigh. "Have you ever tried to undress a corpse?"

"No."

"Neither have I, but I can easily imagine it would be difficult, what with all that slippery gore and goo. All your guys were plastered in blood or their gear was damaged."

"I've got blood on my gear."

"I can wash that off easily enough. Maybe I won't even bother. The more blood, the fewer questions between the time I step out into daylight and the isolation truck. I'm betting nobody will want to come near me."

"If you shoot me, the hole in the suit will ruin your disguise."

"I'd have to shoot you in the foot — or the feet, sure. Then I'd have to leave you here crying while I schlep back to forage for a pair of boots from one of your dead. Honestly, Daniel, this will go smooth and easy if you simply cooperate. I've thought this through and I am smarter than you. We'll end up in the same place. If we do this the easy way, you don't end up wounded and begging me to kill you. I could improvise but I'm on a schedule here."

"A schedule?"

"It's my last day of work and I can't wait to get out of here. I only have to bluff my way to the sidewalk. The isolation truck will be waiting."

"You have an accomplice in the truck."

His casual shrug gave nothing away but the way he widened his eyes told me I'd hit on the truth. *"Sonofabitch.* Who's your guy on the outside? " I took one step toward him.

Hamish raised the pistol to his own head. "Hear me out and consider this, Daniel. Under Yellowstone there is a supervolcano. When it erupts, a vast lake of magma will spew out and send the Earth into a volcanic winter. In the first few minutes, most of North America will die. Soon after, so will everyone else. In geologic time, it's a *certainty* it will happen. Could be in the next few seconds, could be on your birthday, maybe a couple hundred years from now. Nobody knows."

"What the hell is your point?"

"This technology is a supervolcano. Let me do what I have to do to keep it from erupting today and you buy the world some time. My sabotage could set the progression of this work back years. Otherwise, everything you're trying to save will go away in a puff of smoke. No more pizzas, no more M&Ms, no more KISS cover bands. Nothing! No more weddings or honeymoons, no happy times, at all. Everyone you've ever known or could know will die screaming. A shitload of cannibalism will spread across the globe."

"The infection is contained if it's down here."

"The *infestation,*" he corrected me. "Don't worry. My pets in the shower tanks will be dead in a few hours. As long as you don't have a shower immediately after I leave, the waterborne parasites won't be a bother to anyone. They've done their job."

I stared at the hexagonal box. "It's really worth all this death?"

"I should have saved Bob and let them eat you, you idiot. How many people would you kill to save billions of others? One? A dozen? Thousands? Millions? Your bomb disposal specialist did the math. Be like Bob. Do the math and gimme the suit."

Hot tears blurred my vision and slipped down my cheek. "My team is dead. What will I tell their families?"

"That's a bureaucratic problem. Tell them whatever you want if the truth doesn't work. I understand you aren't dealing with bosses who are adept at nuance and moral ambiguity. Consider what happens if I don't get out of here with these organo-nanites? When the end begins, what few survivors there may be will envy the problem of what to say to your bosses. Think it through, Daniel. Everybody's skull is a womb for the Picasso Strain."

"Picasso Strain?"

"That's what they named the worst nanotech ever devised. AFTER was the precursor, the good thing that gave birth to the bad thing. Under a microscope, Picasso's beasties stain blue. We added the pretty coloration so we could identify Picasso's distribution pattern when the micro-monsters are dispersed on air currents. That wasn't the main reason, though. You want to know why they gave a bio-weapon the name Picasso?"

"Well?"

"They consider it a masterpiece. Told you, these people have no souls."

2 8

Hamish had my gun to his head but he held the whole world hostage. *Picasso*. The name filled me with revulsion. They thought their robo-brain parasites that made people into killer zombies was a good thing. *Hmph*. I also didn't want to get shot in the feet or anywhere else.

I put both hands on my hood, hesitated a moment, and pulled it up and off. The respirator clicked closed as I took my last breath from my oxygen tank. As I expected, the facility was awash in the sickly sweet aroma of that industrial cleaner common to hospitals.

"Cheer up, Daniel. You came in here to save the world and you are helping. You're a hero."

"I don't feel like a hero," I said.

"It's a dirty world. I wish we were pulling kids out of burning buildings but reality is seldom so clear-cut. When you're in the middle of a problem, the things you may have to do don't feel heroic. They feel … "

"Necessary?"

"Yeah."

I leaned on the wall, taking a few deep breaths before moving to pull off the rest of my gear. I wasn't up for a fight. Could I mount a defense against Hamish? *Could* was beyond my reach. Should I? I wasn't sure what *should* meant anymore. Hamish made a pretty good argument.

I got my blue biohazard suit off and put it on the floor at Hamish's feet. I wore a t-shirt, shorts and socks. The cool air was a relief. Hamish didn't trust me to stay passive. He ordered me to go to the other end of the locker room while he pulled on my gear. I was fine with that. Whatever happened next, I'd leave Hamish to the guys outside. The rest of the ETF wasn't suffering trauma and concussion. Someone else's decisions got me into the Box. I'd let them figure out what to do about Hamish.

He was halfway into the Hazmat when he pulled a thick roll of duct tape from a cabinet over a sink. Keeping the pistol on me, he instructed me to place several long strips of tape on the counter sticky side up.

I did as I was told but was startled when he opened the hexagonal box. "What are you doing?"

He waved me back with the Glock. I stayed against the far wall, hands up. I had no hope of getting my weapon back. As I stood watching him poke through the box I worried that I had it all wrong. If I was closer, Hamish could shoot me once in the head. I didn't relish the idea. It wouldn't be pleasant but it would be over so quick there wouldn't be time to worry. A headshot at close range would be much quicker than multiple gunshots bursting my organs randomly. How would I die in that scenario? Which awful demise would win in the race between organ failure and blood loss?

"Relax," Hamish said. "These little monsters are sealed in test tubes. They're so hardy, they don't even have to stay cold. As long as they don't aerosolize, we're fine and everybody lives."

"I'd still be more comfortable if you kept them in the big steel box," I said.

"If I'm going to walk out of here, I can't walk out into the summer sunshine looking like a lab rat, now, can I?"

Hamish placed the test tubes along the strips of duct tape and proceeded to awkwardly strap them to his chest. They were invisible under the biohazard suit.

"Is there any kind of security code I should know to tell your superiors as I exit the building?"

I said nothing.

"I have to make it to the isolation truck, Daniel. Remember, my safety is everyone's safety."

"The incident commander's name is Mac," I said. "When you come out, hold the gun up high. Don't point it at anyone. Say, ETF! Two coming out."

"You're Two?"

"Yeah."

"Anything else?"

"If challenged, the security code is 'friendly giant.'"

"Friendly giant? You wouldn't shit a shitter, would you, Daniel?"

"Like you said, your safety is everybody's safety."

"Cool. Thanks, man. You're a real mensch."

He placed the yellow code card on a counter by the sink and told me to read it to him as he stepped to the hatch to Level 1.

I did as I was told. "5 - 5 - A - Z - 2 - 5 - 0 - 0 - L - 1 - 1 - V - 3 - T - P - D - Q."

Hamish keyed it in and cranked open the hatch. He pointed the Glock my way and I returned to my place by the far wall. He picked up the yellow card. "Thanks for all your help."

"I don't think you gave me a whole lot of choice."

"Everything is a choice."

"Until it's not."

"Whatever helps you sleep at night, Daniel."

"I guess this is where we part ways, huh? You going to shoot me now?"

"That won't be necessary."

"You're going to leave me trapped down here."

"If all goes well for me, someone will come down to find out what happened."

"Eventually, maybe, if all goes well. Big ifs, Hamish."

"It'll be fine. I'll leave you here while I walk out the front door like a boss. Get it? Like a boss?" His laugh was a high nasal sound, as if he was squeezing a duck to make it quack in a panic. He waved cheerily as he closed the hatch behind him. I heard the lock click.

I walked slowly around the locker room in a circle. I had two minutes before he cleared the lock and I could challenge the keypad.

5 - 5 - A - Z - 2 - 5 - 0 - 0 - L - 1 - 1 - V - 3 - T - P - D - Q.

"*Fifty-five African Zebras To 500 Lions Won One Victory, Three Trapped People Died Quick.*" Trying to stay steady on my feet, I repeated the word mnemonic over and over, as I paced. That's how I remembered the override code to escape to Level 1.

29

Minutes later I emerged from the hatch on Level 1. I almost caught up with Hamish. He must have hesitated, building up his nerve for the final phase of his plan. Dr. Hamish Allen — savior of the world, scientist with a Jesus complex and concerned father — waved at me as he stepped over the body of the woman in the doorway.

"Daniel! Aren't you clever! I thought I had you locked up good! Can't keep a good man down! Gotta run! Stay down here or I *will* shoot you."

He headed up the ramp to the Box's exit. I didn't doubt he would shoot. He'd come too far to turn back. As he disappeared up the ramp, a stupid inspiration came over me. I still had a way to take him into custody and get my weapon back.

I ran to the office closet. The security guard had run out of blood from his nasty head wound. I scooped up the gun in his lap and checked the cylinder. One shot fired, four rounds to go. I didn't want to fire any. I needed Hamish to put the Glock down. Let Mac figure out the rest while I went on vacation. Maybe I'd go on vacation and never come back. That sounded just fine.

I ran out of the office, leaping over the trampled woman and charging up the ramp. I can't say what made me work so hard to get to him. Part of it was pride. My team was dead and Hamish held my weapon. The rest? All the important questions that so concerned Hamish Allen? To my great shame, I have to admit I wasn't thinking about any of that.

I drove through a snowstorm on the 401 between London, Ontario and Toronto, once. The flurries were thick, the road was ice and the ploughs were insufficient to deal with the quick accumulation of snow. It took hours longer than it should have and the trip was so dangerous I should have pulled off the road and holed up somewhere. I was too stubborn to drive safely. I pressed on, barely able to see more than a couple of car lengths ahead.

Chasing Hamish was that stupid. It was my job to make sure he didn't escape the Box. I tried to do my duty. Besides, I worried that if Mac saw through his disguise, Crenshaw might snipe the bioengineer in the chest. Those test tubes had to remain unbroken and returned to their steel box in the vault. If it came to him or me, I would have to shoot Hamish in the head.

Too late, I dashed past the elevators as Hamish stepped into the sunshine.

"ETF! Two, coming out!" Hamish yelled as I'd told him to do. We were roughly the same height. With the biohazard suit on and the distortion of the hood, Mac would have no reason to doubt it was me walking out of the Box alone.

"Where's the rest of your team, Two?" It was Mac on the bullhorn.

Hamish made a slicing gesture across his throat. Then he pointed to the white isolation van and went down the first step. "Friendly giant, Mac! Friendly giant!"

I stepped to the shadows inside of the doorway and raised the pistol, aiming for a quick clean headshot. "That's far enough, Hamish. It's over now."

"Oh, Daniel. You don't know when to quit."

I cocked the weapon. I knew he heard me. He stiffened and stood taller. "Drop the gun or I'll shoot you through the head."

"But my head is where all the answers are."

"Someone else will figure out what needs to be figured out. I can't let you leave. I don't really know what you'll do with those things. Maybe you'll sell them to North Korea."

"I told you — "

"You told me lots of things. We'll work it out. Now drop the gun."

Hamish dropped my Glock to the steps. I felt a wave of relief wash over me. "Turn around and pull off the hood."

He turned slightly and did as he was told. He gave me a sheepish grin.

"Hands away from your chest. Show me your hands."

"Man, you don't get it." He raised both hands, surrendering peacefully. "Go ahead. Take the little beasties. I tried to save the world but, you know what? It's not worth the effort. I was right. Everybody has a blind spot."

As he turned, Hamish gestured to the street to reveal to me my blind spot. I was so focused on the doctor, I failed to maintain situational awareness. That's a fancy way of saying I focused too much on the wrong problem.

At the bottom of the steps, a long line of bodies lay in the street. Each river of blood draining toward the gutters wound back to a civilian. Mostly they died from head and chest shots. Some must have tried to run when the carnage really got going.

Too many casualties lay in the street for them all to be Echidna employees. There were too many to easily count. The ETF must have lined them up. My colleagues must have ensured their cooperation by ordering them to their knees at gunpoint. They'd promise a safe ride home as soon as they identified everyone. Maybe they told them the isolation truck and a cozy stay in quarantine awaited them over at St. Mike's. Then they shot them all to contain any potential contagion.

There was probably a more sophisticated and less bloody way to solve the problem. Since that moment I have come to understand that everyone favors the quick and easy answer, no matter how blunt and brutal. They could call their crime a terrorist attack. They'd confiscate all surveillance evidence. Even the recordings from the cameras in the ATMs at the bank across the street would disappear. Quick and easy, blunt and brutal. Troubling questions would soon be dismissed as conspiracy theories.

My gaze fell on the woman in white. Her summer dress was mostly red now. Her long red hair, now wet with blood, looked like a hunk of wire. She'd been so pretty and now she was so dead.

In the next minute, I would envy her.

Hamish gave a slow half-turn. "Dude! See how casual they are about killing. They didn't even wait to see if anyone was infested. Your friend was right. We aren't getting out of here. We're all about to enter Picasso's blue period, Dan — "

Mac gave the order to shoot. He didn't kill me. Mac only thought he was murdering me. The sniper got Hamish square in the middle of his skull full of secrets.

Stunned, I stood covered in pink mist from Hamish Allen's brilliant and shattered brain.

The round did not shatter the test tubes strapped to Hamish Allen's chest. Hell was not unleashed upon an unsuspecting planet by a sniper's bullet. The fall down the concrete steps did that. I heard the glass shatter. I inhaled the fine blue mist and the brain parasites did what brain parasites do.

Picasso went to work on me.

30

Mac stepped into the street in a blue Hazmat. I was sure it was him because he carried a bullhorn. He came to a stop behind the corpse of the red-haired woman. He peered into the doorway, surely wondering who was left in the Box. Who had the dead man been talking to, and what was the blue mist rising from the corpse?

All I could think about — if you could call it thinking — was the dead woman at his feet. He didn't spare a glance at her for a second. It was if she did not exist, had never existed. She didn't matter and neither did I. We were merely human sacrifices, no more valuable today than when thousands were massacred a day atop Mayan pyramids.

What had that woman's name been? I groped for the memory. It hadn't even been an hour since I called in her name. I pointed killers her way and she'd been rounded up with the rest for extermination.

Kaela ... Kaela Santini. I remembered because of that movie, *The Great Santini.*

I'd sat at her desk. I'd seen her picture and her password. How soon would she be forgotten as the contagion spread on the wind?

Even those who'd known her, supposing they survived, would soon blur her entire life into an empty statistic. We all blur into history but she was so young and pretty.

Fury overcame my exhaustion then. I'd been sent on a suicide mission, ill-prepared and now, ill. I was sure it wasn't Hamish Allen's "beasties" affecting me, though. Not yet. Despite my concussion, the loss of my squad and the weird parasites that would soon turn me into their killer robot, I was still me. And what could I do with my remaining minutes as Daniel Harmon?

I leaned out of the doorway, raised the security guard's .38 and fired. I pulled the trigger on Mac as fast as I could. It was a thoughtless and petty act. I'm not proud of it. He wasn't so close that I could nail him easily, but I did manage to empty the weapon before the rest of the ETF opened fire on me.

Taking everyone by surprise, I hit Mac once with the first shot, high on the left shoulder. He spun sideways and went down. The rest of my shots went high and wide. I ducked back as numerous rounds chunked the concrete and glass around the front door. I dashed close along the lobby wall, out of the line of fire. Panting, I dove over the security desk.

I wondered if the gremlins in my head would go to work on me faster if my heart beat fast and increased my blood circulation. Did it matter? Either way, I'd turn into one of those unthinking animals, ravenous and hopelessly cruel.

I got up on my knees. The surveillance cameras were still working. I saw three of my fellow ETF officers rush forward with shields, weapons up and trained on the front door.

"Doesn't matter now, you dumb shits," I said. "I'll go first but Mac's next. You're all next."

Blue mist, Picasso nanites, beasties … whatever you are, do your worst.

That's the moment I realized I'd made a tactical error. In my anger, I'd failed to save a bullet for myself. Of course, the guys outside seemed pretty eager to oblige in the Suicide by Cop Department. I had something important to do first. I sprinted back down the ramp to the office on Level 1.

How much time before the mix of advanced microscopic

machines and primitive brain parasites erased my consciousness and turned me into a killer zombie?

If I'd known what was about to happen, I would have run to kneel beside Kaela and take the shot. I'd have accepted death's erasure gladly.

Would have ... could have ... should have ... didn't.

31

Back on the ramp to the Level 1 offices, I leaned hard on the wall, panting. No time for regrets now, I pushed off and left a long bloody smear as I staggered back to Kaela Santini's desk.

My head pounded. I thought I might vomit but I'd felt that way since that big guy bounced my head off the floor. Were these symptoms of what was or what was to come? Would I fall into a quick coma first? Or, much worse, would I *feel* my mind slipping away? What would my last memory be?

My earliest and most tenuous memory is seeing my own hands in front of me as I crawled across a vinyl floor. The floor's pattern was fake brick. My mother told me that was the kitchen in our old house so I might have been two years old. Would that be the first memory to be erased? How long before I became a drooling animal?

My father was diagnosed with early onset Alzheimer's at fifty-four. To him, the worst part of the disease is seeing the end come too slowly. He doesn't believe in God. However, when his morning crossword puzzle became a twisted mystery in another language, he began to pray for a quick heart attack. To ebb away and not be himself anymore? He calls his fate, "Cruel and not unusual enough."

Dad is still alive. Aside from putting random items in the fridge, he's been doing better than the doctors expected. (I once found the TV remote in the meat drawer.) I wondered if the tiny machines spreading on the blue mist would find a home in my father's head, too. Would they find his decaying brain hospitable? Or would he simply fall victim to a random attack and be eaten alive?

Not as fast as a heart attack but faster than Alzheimer's, I thought. *Maybe Dad won't mind so much.*

It was a grim thought, so I shoved it aside. I could still do something useful. I plopped into Kaela's chair and opened her drawer to see her password again: *3BearsDoGoldilocks.*

Kaela, you were a funny woman. I'm sure we would have gotten along. I'm sorry I helped murder you.

I touched the mouse and her screen came alive. I logged in with her password. The screen changed and I found she'd been looking at a travel site. She'd been planning a trip to the tropics when the alarm sounded. She'd been comparing prices of resorts in Cancun and the Dominican Republic. I wanted to stare at those pictures and imagine myself in places I'd never been. There wasn't time.

I clicked a tab that took me to her gmail page. I clicked on *COMPOSE* and prayed I'd remembered my sister's email address properly. I would have called her but the phones didn't work. Without my cell, I had no idea what her number was.

JENN,

I'VE MESSED UP. You were right. I should have become a physiotherapist. I don't know how much time I have but as soon as you see this, run. Get as far away from Toronto as you can. Maybe up north. Find weapons and, this is going to be hard but leave dad. Ggo I can"t expll —

·   ·   ·

...

ICANT EXPLHOGSDSD —

...

(DEEP BREATH.)

I I PIƷHAFS —
O[isƒjosƒjsfsvsof[pkk [kj[pÿjsfd ...

MY FINGERS WOULDN'T DO what I wanted. I managed to click send. That was all. I stared at the screen, the keyboard and my traitorous hands.

Damn it. I knew I should have chosen my last words ahead of time! Something pithy and concise would have been better.

I sat for some time waiting and thinking about the decisions, turns and accidents that had led me to this chair. I thought of the cheating girlfriend who told me I'd look sexy in uniform. Had my decision to become a cop truly been based on that? Not entirely. But without that specific encouragement, I wouldn't have done it at all. I could be a thousand miles from here and oblivious to the danger blowing in the wind, multiplying in God knew how many brains. Was Mac getting patched up by a paramedic at that same moment? Was he staring at a name tag or a sign and wondering why the letters didn't make sense?

I didn't break up with that girlfriend because she steered me wrong. I didn't even break up with her because she cheated. As many relationships go, ours wobbled back and forth a few times before it toppled over. I eventually broke it off because she told me I should work for my dad in that last summer before college ended. I wanted to take a road trip to California. She told me to grow up and make some money instead. That's what finally tore it up for me.

The irony is, I didn't go on that road trip of my dreams. I did work for my father moving heavy things around a warehouse for one more torturous summer. I'd worked in that dank warehouse since I was thirteen. I took on part-time jobs to try to pay for my own place, to be free and independent. I remained chained.

Even as the parasites wormed their way deeper, through the meat and juice of my brain, my mind suddenly felt clearer. My epiphany was this: I'd been going the wrong way for years. I had been free once and it was as a child. The last day of summer when I was twelve was the last time I'd known real happiness. After that, it was all work, worry and striving.

What and when is enough? When can we stop having to prove ourselves? And what are we proving?

I was tired of trying so damn hard. It came to nothing much anyway. I guess grim realizations are what people think about on their deathbeds. I looked down and realized where I was. I wouldn't die on clean white sheets. No death bed for me. I got a death office chair instead.

The cheating girlfriend went back to my former best friend who was studying to become a chiropractor. I guess none of that matters. Soon there would be only two jobs: hunters and prey. Maybe getting my mind erased wouldn't be so bad. Zombies pay no taxes. Becoming a dumb animal could be a solid stress management strategy.

I saved a little boy from drowning in Lake Ontario once. That was the best thing I ever did and I wasn't even on duty. I didn't think about it. I just dove in and pulled him out. His mom stalked across the beach, yanked the kid to his feet and swore at him all the way back to the parking lot. He was too busy crying to look at me. His mom didn't even thank me. That was one of the best days out of a lot of shitty ones. It was pure.

Then came the Emergency Task Force, another nail in my coffin. We'd come in as a unit, so strong. When Mac ordered us to flatten to get out of the line of fire, we'd all dropped to the deck as if we were one person. We came into the Box with purpose and confidence, weapons ready and geared up to be faceless, nameless Hazmat heroes. I didn't think of us as people with first names. We had numbers. We must have looked so badass when we came through the front door.

Only when we failed and fell, one by one, did we become humans with names again. Lundsden became Bob. Taylor became Steve. Davis became Patrick. I was just Daniel now.

Bob, Steve, Patrick, Danny. Little boys' names.

And our fearless leader, Frank Barnes, became the son of a bitch who led us into Hell blind.

It is strange how personal death is. People die in great masses on the news, and it's a blip in our consciousness, noted and soon forgotten. It's not a tragedy until it's personal.

I was about to find out there really are worse things than death. Dad would have understood the horror that was about to crush me. However, understanding a thing doesn't necessarily make it better. Sometimes ignorance really is bliss.

When I was in training, an instructor asked my class, "Is it better to be smart or brave?" He went around the room, pinning my classmates down on an answer.

When he came to me, I answered with a joke, "Brave. I can do brave things but I'm only as smart as I'm ever going to be."

The instructor had the grace to laugh. Then he told us why smart was better. "If you're smart, you won't have to be so brave." By smart, he really meant *careful*.

I have a different answer now. It's better to be brave. Smart people did this to me.

32

The hunger hit me in the pit of my stomach, as harsh as a body blow. *Pang* is not the right word. *Pain* is the word. I'd never been so hungry in my life. I was ravenous.

I fell from the chair and gripped the floor with my toes and fingers as if the room might turn upside down at any moment. The carpet felt very rough under my hands, as if the texture suddenly had more depth. The carpet was not a flat plane, anymore, not to me. It was as nuanced as a topographical model of a mountain range. I saw new patterns in the rug and felt the contours in its patterns.

Colors became more vivid, too. My vision sharpened to a focus that made my eyeballs dry and hot. I could see the smudges of fingerprints and handprints on the computer screens and desks. My stomach tightened to a knot.

Palm prints. Fingerprints. Everywhere we go we leave a sheen of oil, sweat and dust. I could see it and smell it. There was a tang in the air. The smell revolted my mind but enticed my body.

We have all seen zombie movies. They range from comedy to horror and back again. In almost all the outbreak scenarios, the infected were hungry monsters. Fast or slow, zombies were mindless animals. Under attack, I'd certainly thought of them that way. Near death and dealing with a hundred terrors, much had slipped past me. Then I remembered the attacker who'd nearly killed me, the one who seemed to mouth the words, *"I'm sorry, I'm sorry. I'm sorry."*

In the melee, I'd dismissed that thought as a battlefield reaction. On my hands and knees, muscles coiling and flexing, ready to spring, I knew what came next. I understood what I would do. I couldn't stop what was about to happen. I couldn't even scream.

I raised my head and sniffed the air.

Oh, no, oh, no, oh, no, no, no ...

My muscles flexed. I stalked forward on all fours. As the spectrum of my senses expanded, my body felt more powerful than ever. Even as the ache throbbed in the pit of my empty stomach, there was a strange ecstasy in this new flood of feelings.

My body felt very alive but I wanted desperately to be dead inside. I wanted to scream, *"Do what you want with my brain! Take it all! Take the last part of me that's still here and kill it."*

Instead, I turned my attention to the scents wafting from the closet, more enticing than any aroma of baking bread. Better than Christmas turkey with stuffing and mashed potatoes in gravy. A feast waited for me in the closet.

No, no, no, no, no!

When I was the old Daniel Harmon, I'd often meet people who got uptight when they found out I was a cop. I'd wander around a party and a stranger would turn into a bleeding heart before my eyes. These people seemed both privileged and well-meaning. They weren't good listeners, though. They'd never had to deal with real trouble in a physical way. If they got mugged or became a victim, they'd call someone like me to deal with it.

Despite their lack of experience on the street, they'd whine about how police treated criminals. They'd talk about the tragedy of imprisoning lawbreakers. "Drug addiction is a social issue, not a legal one," they'd say. They'd call the courts our "injustice system." Then they'd complain about economic disparity, disenfranchisement and blah, blah, blah.

Typically, I'd respond with something like, "If all you say is true, why aren't *all* poor people thieves, drug addicts and violent assholes? Why give the worst of us a free pass?"

In the time it took me to knock back another beer, I'd get an earnest lecture on why people did things for reasons they didn't understand, reasons beyond their control. They'd bang on about chronic institutionalization, bad parenting, bad genes and bad brains.

I'd wait patiently. When the stranger ran out of steam, I'd say, "I can only judge people by what they do."

Then I'd walk away in search of the comfort of someone who agreed with me. Somebody once said that's the definition of genius: anyone who agrees with you.

I'd only just discovered that I wasn't in control of much of anything, not since that last day of summer when I was twelve. I was too busy following orders. I'd worked hard, but was it for what I wanted? Or was my life merely a tribute to what other people expected?

With saliva dripping from my mouth, panting like a dog, I was out of control. I certainly wouldn't want to be judged by what I did next.

The dead security guard waited for me in the closet. The trampled woman in the doorway was good for another meal or two. My body had a new and grisly addiction.

In an Intro Psych class, I'd once listened to a professor argue with a student about what they both called "the Observer."

The student posed the idea that there was a presence in the back of each mind, something or someone watching our thoughts bubble up. The student said that was God watching us.

The professor shut him down hard and said something I didn't understand about "infinite regression," and the subconscious mind. They talked a long time about stuff nobody really understands. I dropped that course because I didn't think those people had any answers.

Now I am the Observer. In this dark place, I have a lot of time to think. I go over and over all my mistakes, indecisions and bad decisions. I don't have any answers, just more questions. Maybe the point is that there is no point. I hate that answer, so I go over everything again only to arrive at the same non-conclusion.

I fell upon the security guard's corpse. As I tore at his uniform to get at his throat and soft belly, my mind reeled in horror.

This isn't me. This isn't me. This isn't me!

I saw every revolting movement of my arms and hands. I tasted the meat in my mouth as I ripped and chewed. I felt the man's blood slide down my throat as I drank from his jugular.

I can feel shame and experience horror but I am a passenger. I used to be in the driver's seat but my bus is on ice, no brakes. My mind's commands can't reach my body. I can do nothing to stop myself from doing terrible things.

This isn't me!

I am not dead. I am still in this body, alive and terrified. I watch, out of control and hating what happens. My father would understand this feeling. He knows what it feels like to slip away, to lose yourself, to become someone else.

Even if I could be cured, could anyone forgive me? Whatever magic the combination of parasites and techno-wizardry Hamish's research team had wrought, it changed me into a thing, a tool, a weapon, a killer robot. I am not evil, but I am in a living hell. Death's erasure would have been so merciful.

I wish I could tell people this thing I've become is not me. I am my own evil twin. In hindsight, maybe that's a little true of all of us. Every dark impulse comes from a place we don't recognize or understand. I am a victim who looks and acts like a predator.

Who am I? Who was I?

Once a flawed human being, I am now a meat puppet. Trapped. This perfect murder machine — so singular of purpose — wears my face. My thoughts are all I have now. I am a zombie made from brain parasites and microscopic machines. Daniel Harmon is dead but this is not the afterlife. This is my AFTER life.

AFTERWORD

In October 2016, the Obama White House issued a report called *Preparing for the Future of Artificial Intelligence.* Under the Safety and Control section, you'll find the following quote:

"If (AI) practitioners cannot achieve justified confidence that a system is safe and controllable, so that deploying the system does not create an unacceptable risk of serious negative consequences, then the system cannot and should not be deployed. A major challenge ... is building systems that can safely transition from the 'closed world' of the laboratory into the outside 'open world' where unpredictable things can happen."

THIS IS THE END OF BOOK ONE

Books live and die by reviews.
If you dig my sling, please leave a happy review wherever
you purchased this book.

∼

Curious about what comes next in the NEXT apocalypse?
Turn the page for a sneak peek at

AFTER Life

PURGATORY

AFTER Life

PURGATORY

～

In this prison we call home,
every heart will turn to stone
These cages of flesh and bone,
rise in heat,
burn fast
and too quickly cool.
Not much mercy, more the fool,
let out a brave laugh.
to untether your tears
We are only more than we appear
when we grow larger
than each fear.

D ANIEL

I FED on the guard's body first. I'd seen the movie in which a bunch of soccer players resorted to cannibalism in the mountains. This wasn't like that. It was as if I were watching a very realistic and gory video game from the first person perspective. Some*thing* else was at the controls. The weaponized brain parasites wriggled in my brain, taking over and telling my body what to do. I was no longer Daniel Harmon, Emergency Task Force officer. Unfortunately, I wasn't the dead variety of zombie, either. My actions were no longer my own.

I watched as I yanked the clothes of the dead aside to get at the meat. I dove for the soft parts first: the throat and abdomen. Ears are chewy and tough. It's easier to tear meat from the finger bones than I would have thought.

I wanted to throw up but I couldn't. My revulsion was alive but my objections remained intellectual and unheard. I would have screamed if I could. Instead, I ate and, despite the gore and my disgust, my body was ravenous.

Someone told me once that if you don't stop a dog from feeding, they'll simply keep eating until they die (like what happens with people, but quicker.) That's how it was with me, feeding off the carcasses on Level 1 of the Box.

I was not totally divorced from my body. That was the confusing part. I could feel everything but I could not change anything. I felt no desire for my grisly meal but I did taste every wet morsel. I couldn't vomit. Instead, I could chew hungrily. To a starving man, a spleen is the same as Black Forest cake. A casual bystander would surely conclude I was enjoying myself.

As if in the thrall of some strange drug, I felt stronger with every bite. Energy pulsed through me. My skin tingled and my muscles felt full, cranked high with kinetic potential like tight steel springs. I moved with an ease that made me feel I'd finally be a threat on the basketball court. If only zombies played basketball.

I heard screams from far away, up the ramp and out in the sunshine. I was curious what was going on in Toronto's streets. I guess my brain parasites were interested, too. I lifted my head from the large woman before me, leapt to my feet, and ran up the ramp.

I didn't kill the woman or the security guard I ate, I thought. *Someone else had murdered them. The next murdered meal is on me. So far, my crime was "committing an indignity to a dead person."*

I knew a cop who had arrested a naked sicko in a cemetery on that charge. Now I'd join the ranks of the sickos. Whatever was in control of my body wasn't a person I could argue with. I didn't receive a message or hear a voice. I sensed no ghostly presence. I ran, working on automatic, empty of volition. It is a curious thing to be carried along on a wave. I felt like a passenger and the thing that was controlling my body was a hit and run driver.

As I emerged from the Box and onto the downtown street, I guessed what the brain parasites wanted: live prey, fresh meat. The robotic brain parasites infesting my skull wanted to chase someone. The zombies in the Box acted like wolves and I was a member of the pack.

To my left, the ETF's biohazard isolation truck was parked on the curb. The engine was still running. To my right, executed bodies lay in a line, bloodied and still. Beyond those dead lay many more.

And there were people like me. The infested were on their hands and knees, bending to their awful work, ripping, tearing and chewing. Downtown Toronto was a war zone. The humans had already lost the battle and the infection was spreading fast.

No, I'd been told *infection* was wrong. Hamish preferred *infestation*. A super parasite powered by microscopic robots was an *infestation*. Or maybe it was more accurate to say zombies had infested Toronto. Did that distinction really matter now? Not to me and not to the parasites. They only wanted to feed and reproduce.

So this is how the world ends, I thought. *When the aliens finally came down to Earth to check us out, they'd find a bunch of carnivorous apes that once wore clothes.*

But what would come after that? Would the zombies form tribes or herds? What would happen after the food ran out? By food, I mean the kind of meal who runs around screaming in terror and used to have dreams of owning a cottage by a lake. Would zombies end up devouring each other? Probably. Brain parasites weren't worried about contributing to a healthy human future where we could continue to enjoy trenchant HBO dramas and share amusing cat memes on Facebook.

Then I spotted her across the street: My prey was a woman clothed in a torn blue uniform. She wore a gas mask. She carried a riot shield and a police baton. The mask obscured all her features except her hair, frizzy and matted with sweat. She must have lost her helmet.

I willed my body not to join the hunt. I didn't want to go after her, to climb on her back and smash her to the street, to feed. They say that if you don't want a wild animal to chase you down, don't run. That didn't matter. I would have gone after her even if she managed a casual stroll, I'm sure.

I experienced bodily ecstasy on par with orgasm as I sprinted after my intended victim. I'd never taken PCP, but maybe that experience would be similar. It felt that good to run, to stretch out into long loping strides. I'd never run so fast or hated myself more. I may as well have been shouting down a well for all the good my silent screams did.

She headed for the isolation truck. Powerless to stop myself, I sprinted so hard the air pumping through my lungs felt like an ice cold drink of water on a hot day. Blood thrummed in my ears. I drooled in anticipation.

The woman saw me coming, climbed in the back, and yanked the door to the isolation truck shut behind her. Trucks meant to contain hazardous materials don't lock from the inside. We lock in the threats from the outside. I grabbed the handle, threw the door open and leaped in. When I played basketball, my vertical was never this strong. I bashed into her riot shield and kept pushing to slam my victim into the compartment wall. The truck rocked beneath us as I struggled to get past the shield.

That's it! Keep that shield up! Keep it between us! I'm on your side! I'm so sorry about this. I'm not driving my own bus, here. I'm so sorry!

But I was sure that, in the end, I'd kill her.

CHLOE

I WANDERED through the milling crowd with a bottle of wine. The plan was to take this opportunity to meet the movers and shakers at the bio-cyber symposium. It was easier to have something to do instead of hanging out alone waiting for people to come to me.

Then a thin guy in a ridiculously shiny suit called out to me, "Wine girl? Oh, wine girl!"

I stiffened and slapped on a smile before turning to face him. He sat at the edge of the party with a large man in a cheap, ill-fitting suit. "My name is Chloe, actually! Chloe Robinson!"

"Chloe Actually! C'mere!" He raised his empty glass higher and jiggled it back and forth as if he was ringing a little bell. "I prefer 'wine girl!'"

Moron. I knew trying to be social was a shitty idea.

Thomas Dill, my boss, had told me that mingling with people after the afternoon session on medical applications for nanotech would be good for me and the company. "Make more connections. Meet more people than you would just standing around."

"I do some of my best thinking when I'm 'just standing around.'" I objected. "Besides, they'll see me as a waitress. I was a waitress in university and hated it. That's why I'm here, to get away from drunks pinching my ass."

"No one will pinch your ass. I'm simply suggesting you find a way to be a little more…approachable. You know…friendly."

"I am friendly."

"You're intimidating."

"If they're intimidated, that sounds like an Other People Problem."

"You run your own lab," Thomas said, "but connecting with colleagues and clients is part of the job, too."

"People aren't my forte. I'd rather just climb into a box and think for a few years."

"You're the youngest woman to ever hold your position at this company. Your role carries responsibilities — "

"Sounds to me like you should have promoted other young women a long time ago, then."

Thomas let out a long-suffering sigh. "A little flexibility and gratitude thrown my way would not be amiss, don't you think?"

"Gratitude? I produce results. It's an exchange. I bring a lot to the table. Yours is a suspicious proposition, Thomas."

"I don't mean to say I'm proposing — "

"Propositioning."

"Maybe you missed your calling as a lawyer, Chloe."

"If you're accusing me of being argumentative, it's only because you're giving me something I have to contend with."

Thomas cleared his throat and began again. "I flew you to Aruba with the best of intentions. I'm hoping to forge alliances and develop new accounts so — "

"The conference is shit, Thomas, but I am looking forward to hearing the Foo Fighters play. I saw a clip of Dave Grohl online doing an excellent Christopher Walken impression. Have you seen that? Grohl is the man! He's amazing."

"Why exactly is this multimillion dollar conference shit?"

"It's July in Aruba so it's hot as balls. I should be onstage talking about how my division is developing AI to optimize human hormonal performance. Instead, all these venture capitalists seem to be interested in is weapons development. These guys will be on their deathbed fretting about Islamic extremists while they die of prostate cancer. My work might cure that someday. I don't think there will ever be a cure for terrorism."

"Okay, okay." Thomas gave a smile that was supposed to placate me. "What you don't seem to understand is our weapons division funds your research."

"Short-term, long-term, I get the math. I'm good at cost-benefit analyses. It's what tells me I should be back at the lab instead of mixing with the fancy people."

"You're making me wish you were back at the lab. This is an opportunity to network. You want to talk to other researchers but it's the people with the purse strings you need to court first."

"Courting. That's an interesting turn of phrase."

"These are important people, Chloe."

"Like the guy from Dubai — Mr. Tarkasian? He's the one who asked if I was sleeping with you."

"Oh? What did you tell him?"

"I told him what I told you on that subject, Thomas."

"Ah. A hard no."

"I found it easy to say no."

"*Ouch.* What did Tarkasian say?"

"He asked if I was brought along to accommodate new customers."

"Accommodate? Meaning?"

"You know what he meant. I told him the tech I'm working on could save his life but I'd rather watch him die."

"Chloe! Jesus!"

"I came here to work and to dance to *The Pretender*. No time for assholes."

"I should have left you in your lab. You could have listened to Foo Fighters on Spotify."

When he invited me to the Aruba conference, Thomas told me a bright light from every department would be attending. In the end, I was the only woman on the company jet and I only saw a couple of other department heads. The situation didn't sit well but I'd dealt with this sort of thing before. The head of Human Resources was on my speed dial if the flirting leveled up to anything I considered dangerous. My work was valuable to the company and I wasn't afraid to speak up. Thomas knew not to push me too far. They didn't want to lose my input and they definitely didn't want a lawsuit.

"Wine girl!"

Which brings me back to the thin guy in the shiny suit.

"Where've you been all my life, wine girl? I'm thirsty!"

137

"Chloe Robinson, with Prometheus Rembrandt BioSystems," I said.

"Prometheus Rembrandt. *Heh*. When companies merge, the juxtapositions can really come out ridiculous, can't they?"

"Do you want white wine?" I asked.

"White, yes."

I hefted the bottle. "That's a tragedy, I've only got red."

"You'll find a bottle of white over by the bar, honey." He brayed and looked to his silent companion. The large moon faced man was probably worth a billion but dressed like a flood victim. Though he was deep into middle age, his cheeks were marred with acne. I felt sorry for him. He wore a tragically lopsided toupee and I guessed he had no friends to tell him the truth about his artificial hair.

The big man glanced up at me a second. Our eyes met and he looked away quickly. I suddenly liked him quite a bit. He seemed to have the good sense to be embarrassed by his companion.

I took a deep breath and let it out slowly. Then I sat beside the man in the shiny suit. "What's your name, 'honey?'" I asked.

"A name you should already know. My company does enough business with yours — "

"Uh-huh. I guess you're not as famous as you think."

It was his turn to stiffen. "We are one of your company's best customers. Why don't you go fetch me that drink and we'll talk about it?"

I was furious, of course. My rage was made worse because Thomas appeared before I had a chance to call the man out on his shenanigans. My boss did not look pleased but I gave him a bright smile. I could afford to be sassy. AFTER was the next generation of technology that could save the world. I didn't understand then how urgently the world needed saving.

DANIEL

I watched as my left hand curled around the top of the riot shield.

The cop smashed my fingers with her baton. It hurt, but not as much as it should have. I tried again, faster. She attempted to smash my fingers but I was too quick for her the second time. I wrenched the shield away. She pulled the pistol from her holster and almost managed to point it at my gut. I slapped the Glock 22 out of her hand before she could pull the trigger.

I wondered what she would taste like. Had she showered recently? What if she had hepatitis or lyme disease? Would I contract it, too? If the microscopic parasites were airborne, how many people would get the disease? Would I eat her or would I bite her to make her like me? The world had changed in the space of an hour and a half. What were the new rules?

My right hand flashed out and grabbed my victim by the throat. She struck my elbow with the baton and it stung badly, as if a thousand bees buzzed up my arm.

I lunged, jaws snapping, and she recoiled with such force that she bashed her own head against the wall. She didn't drop the baton but her grip loosened enough that prying the weapon from her fingers was no more difficult than taking a stick from a determined child.

I had her. All I had to do was grab her throat again and close my fist. Then I would feed. I would feed the parasites running my brain and, if I concentrated really hard, maybe I could mouth the word *sorry* between bites.

She dropped to the truck's floor and I followed to bring my weight down, intent on pinning her. I would have killed her then but she still wore the gas mask. To my surprise, she reached for a can of mace that had been ready on the floor. She sprayed me in the face and I reeled back just as I spotted two more cops climbing into the back, riot shields held high, bearing down on me.

Two darts pierced my chest. Taser. All my muscles stiffened in torturous spasms. I fell to the deck. My fellow officers began to beat me down. *Good for them.*

The pain was bad. I waited patiently for the feeling that I was beginning to go away. It did not come quickly or easily. They hit me across the back, butt and legs too much and not enough in the head.

They grunted with the effort, swinging their batons hard. I lived, impatient to die.

Someone's knee came down on the back of my neck. As I stared out the back of the truck I saw someone in a silver asbestos suit shooting a thirty-foot arm of fire from a flamethrower. Joint Task Force 2 must have arrived to incinerate the bodies in the street, torching the evidence of how the world began to end. As the man with the flamethrower burned the bodies, a sickly sweet smell permeated the air. The bad smell came from burnt hair. The sweet smell wafted up from the cooking bodies. Cannibals didn't care if their meals were raw or cooked, but the smell and noise might attract more zombies back to the Epicenter of the outbreak.

I saw an amazing thing then. Startled, the man with the flamethrower looked up as a cannibal ran straight at him. It was a young woman, tall and athletic. By the way she pumped her arms as she sprinted, I had the feeling that she might have been a track star. Muscle memory is strong.

The guy with the flamethrower turned his weapon on his attacker. From ten feet out, she caught the flames straight in the face. The first thing a flamethrower does is burn off oxygen. The victim burns second. First, they asphyxiate. The woman had enough air to scream and leap.

I watched her attack unfold as if watching a movie in slow motion. Her scream echoed around the canyon formed by the office building. Her clothes were on fire and burning off her body. The arc of her leap put her above the flame. The man was too slow to react. In a movement as graceful as any Olympic athlete, she crashed into him with both feet to his chest.

He stumbled back and fell over a corpse. She was still burning as she ripped the hood from his head and tore through the thin skin of his throat and into the carotid. She only went down when someone shot her with a heavy calibre machine gun.

Seeing it all in slow motion, I had time to watch and think. I noticed the moment the hunter became the hunted. I felt the defiance in the scream of the attacker. That was not pain or anguish in her voice. That was a war cry full of power. There was something incongruous, a nuance I never would have sensed before. The cannibal's attack was a noble failure, so visceral and wild in its abandon. On the force, we always dehumanized our enemies. Here, in diseased attackers who were already barely human, I felt something new stir in me. For the first time I touched the possibility of respecting an enemy.

The harsh bite of steel cut into my wrists. I heard the ratcheting click of handcuffs secured far too tightly. The beating continued. I closed my eyes and accepted my punishment gratefully. I'd failed my mission. I deserved this.

Soon I'll lapse into unconsciousness. Then I'll be dead for real. Thank you.

This is not the apocalypse anyone expected. Endings are tricky that way. Every civilization stumbles, teeters and falls to ashes, dust and ruin. Everyone and everything falls out of memory. The surprise is that we are at all surprised.

Darkness enveloped me. *This is death,* I thought. *It's not so bad, but if I'm dead, who is thinking that death isn't so bad?*

I'd hoped I'd fade out while dreaming of my first girlfriend. She didn't wear lipstick but she wore cherry lip balm. I loved to watch her put it on and I loved the taste of cherries as I kissed it from her lips. *Cherry lip balm.* I could dream for a moment but it might feel like a thousand years if I could just hold onto that cherished memory until I blacked out and went wherever dead people go.

Anything was preferable to obsessing over the taste of the raw meat from the security guard's guts. A bright white light popped on above me but it wasn't the light at the end of a tunnel we hear of from near-death experiences. People joke about being dead on the inside. That was the hell of it: I was alive, but only on the inside.

THE ACTION CONTINUES IN BOOKS
TWO & THREE

AFTER Life

PURGATORY

&

AFTER Life

PARADISE

IF YOU ENJOY APOCALYPTIC FICTION...

Citizen Second Class

Life's not fair. It's our job to make it that way.
In an eerily familiar near-future, America has fallen to fascism.
Citizenship is attainable only through military service or immense
wealth. The Resistance is broke and broken. Amid this dystopian
landscape, New Atlanta has become a fortress reserved for the
billionaire elite.

Hopes to save the nation have faded but Kismet Beatriz
remains defiant. The intrepid young survivor embarks on a
desperate mission to storm the castle of the Select Few. To win, she
must face the future without flinching.

Don't hope. *Do.*

Amid Mortal Words

A dangerous stranger met on a train leaves behind a powerful book.
With mere words, this book could destroy the world or save it. This

power is now in the hands of one man relying on a mysterious woman to guide him toward the apocalypse or away from our destruction. It's a roller coaster ride filled with twists and turns toward a surprising conclusion that will keep you up all night reading.

This Plague of Days

What will you do to protect your family in the zombie apocalypse? Young Jaimie Spencer is an unlikely hero amid the ashes and ruins of our world. On the spectrum and selectively mute, he's more obsessed with his dictionary than with the fate of humanity. However, before this epic story is over, Good will do battle with Evil and Jaimie is our champion.

Robert's most successful series to date, *This Plague of Days* won Honorable Mention from *Writers' Digest*.

All three seasons of this trilogy are available as an omnibus or individually as ebooks or paperbacks on Amazon.

AFTER Life

Zombies will soon invade the United States. Which side will you join, the infected or the damned?

Artificial Facilitation Therapy for Enhanced Response (AFTER), was a biomimetic stem cell nanotechnology with numerous health and wellness applications. Then a military contractor weaponized it using brain parasites. When the zombie apocalypse we soon discover that genetically engineered zombies are hard to kill.

Officer Daniel Harmon is tasked with stopping the epidemic. Dr. Chloe Robinson needs to get her creation back under control. We can't always get what we want.

IF YOU ENJOY APOCALYPTIC FICTION...

The *AFTER Life* trilogy is available now on Amazon as ebooks or in paperback.

Robot Planet

The robots are unfailingly polite until the moment they kill you. This future isn't merely a forbidding dystopia. It's cyberpunk scary.

In this series of four novellas, three very different people join forces to combat the rise of the Next Intelligence. The odds are against us.

Start your next adventure by grabbing *Robot Planet, The Complete Series*, available at Amazon in paperback or ebook.

Haunting Lessons

This is not a ghost story. It only begins that way.

Tamara is a young woman from the Midwest who experiences an unspeakable tragedy. Soon she sees apparitions. That's only the beginning of her adventures. Running away to New York, she soon discovers a secret world of dark magic doing combat with alien forces from another dimension.
If she is to save the world from the coming invasion, Tam must train to become a leader among the Choir Invisible. She fights for us all.

Death Lessons, Fierce Lessons and *Dream's Dark Flight* are also part of this series of gripping adventures.

All Empires Fall

How will the world end?

In this short story collection, Robert shares several tales of the apocalypse. It comes in flood and fire. It stabs at us out of the darkness of space.

Robert Chazz Chute many dark ideas for you to consider and revel in as you stay up through the night turning pages to each ending of our world.

You will a complete listing of the author's books on the next page.

Machines Dream of Metal Gods

(First in the *Robot Planet Series*,

only 99 cents!)

Robot Planet, The Complete Series

All Empires Fall: Signals from the Apocalypse

(anthology)

THE DIMENSION WAR SERIES

Haunting Lessons

Death Lessons

Fierce Lessons

Dream's Dark Flight

~ TIME TRAVEL ~

Wallflower

~ COLLECTIONS ~

Murders Among Dead Trees

Self-help for Stoners

~ NON-FICTION ~

Do the Thing

The Last Stress-busting Book You'll Ever Need

ABOUT THE AUTHOR

Robert Chazz Chute is a former journalist and winner of eight writing awards. He writes apocalyptic epics and killer crime thrillers from Other London.

Find out more at AllThatChazz.com.

For inquiries, contact:
expartepress@gmail.com

Would you like a character named after you?

Immortality is possible.
Randomly selected members of the Facebook page Fans of Robert Chazz Chute will be offered a spot in future novels.

Just want to be alerted when more adventures hit?
Join up for email updates at
AllThatChazz.com.

www.ingramcontent.com/pod-product-compliance
Lightning Source LLC
Chambersburg PA
CBHW050856180626
46814CB00007B/2770